MW00874873

Cassie's Gold

Written by:

Barbara Sue Sweetwood

Sunflower Prairie Publications

Sunflower Prairie Publications

A young Virgil and Cassie Hollister leave their home in Jackson, Mississippi in attempts to find their fortune during the "Gold Rush" in 1850. They hook up with a wagon train in Independence, Missouri and after a long and perilous journey finally make their way to California. There they find hardship, dangerous Indians and surprises around every corner. Is it all worth finding "Cassie's Gold"?

Barbara Sue Sweetwood

To Hatchet Jan,
Glad to be your HCR
neighbor!
Barbara Sue Smithwood
8/14/15

This book is dedicated to all of the men and women that made their way across an untamed and treacherous west in search of a dream and a better life. Many prospectors lost their lives along the trails and many died penniless trying to find that one perfect "gold strike". Although they knew their chances were slim they had the fortitude and tenacity to strike out on a perilous adventure. These brave men and women were part of the foundation that formed these United States into the great country it is today.

Barbara Sue Sweetwood

Cassie's Gold

Author:

Barbara Sue Sweetwood

Copyright ©Barbara Sue Sweetwood 2014

Published by Sunflower Prairie Publications, Kansas

ISBN-13: 978-1494992880

ISBN-10: 1494992884

Edited, designed and formatted by Barbara Sue Sweetwood.

Sunflower Prairie Publications

Read other books by Barbara Sue Sweetwood:

One Woman's Courage - Copyright © 2012

A Rapid Heartbeat -   Copyright © 2012

Emma Woods -   Copyright © 2012

One Woman's Courage Part II

Another Mile-   Copyright © 2013

Cassie's Gold-   Copyright © 2014

Chapter 1

The north wind cut through Cassie as she carefully made her way down the side of the slippery mountain. She had no idea that her life would be in such peril when her husband Virgil had talked her into heading out west to look for gold. The year was 1850 and gold fever had affected a lot of people back east and down south who thought they could travel west and strike it rich. Virgil and Cassie had known each other since they were babies when their mamas use to put them in a wash tub together at bath time. They were the same age, give or take a month, and grew up together in a small town right outside of Jackson, Mississippi. They had spent their entire lives with each other so it was no surprise to anyone when they reached a certain age that they married.

Virgil was a medium built fellow with light brown hair and an infectious smile that could turn a female head at the sight of it. Cassie was small in stature with long brown hair and the brightest blue eyes that Virgil had ever seen. They had both past their nineteenth birthdays a few months earlier. The two of them wed when they were sixteen but most folks married around that age in their neck of the woods and some girls as early as twelve or thirteen.

Virgil had decided that he was not going to kill himself in the cotton fields or coal mines back home. They had no children yet but they wanted a large family. Virgil thought if they could go out west and find their fortune at an early age then they would be set for life and they could afford to have all of the babies that they wanted. Cassie was up for anything new that her husband wanted to try. She had always been a little more of a tomboy than her sister's maybe because she had always played with Virgil when she was young. Once he had suggested that they pull up stakes and head for the golden west Cassie couldn't wait to get their wagon loaded and start out on a new adventure. She could see herself wrapped in fancy silk and linen clothing eating fine foods and sipping brandy like people up north in Boston or New York. She pictured her and Virgil sitting in a room full of squeaky clean children and a maid for each one of them. It was fun to think about but the truth of the matter was that now she wondered if they would ever get down that mountain side with their lives let alone with any gold they might find.

Cassie's boots kept sliding off of the slick wet rocks and she wished she had a more solid place to step down to on her descent to safety.

"Cassie are you okay?" Virgil yelled down at his cold and scared wife as she clung to the rope he had tied around her waist in case she lost her footing.

"So far so good Virgil but these rocks are awful slippery. You be mighty careful when you start climbing down, you hear?" Cassie replied.

"I hear you honey," Virgil hollered down towards his shivering wife.

This trip had not been what either one of them had expected. The cloudless sun shiny afternoons with a skip in their step and a whistle on their lips stopped shortly after the first couple of days. The rains came and practically drowned both of them at their camp site and the winds blew until Cassie's face was wind burnt red and chapped. It was cold in the mountains and there was something around every corner that either wanted to eat you or just wanted you dead. One slip was all it took for you to plummet down the mountain side to certain death. This was an adventure that they both wished they had not embarked on. It was, too late for regrets now and they had to figure out a way to get down from the mountain with their possessions and all of their bones intact.

Cassie had a strong will and stubbornness about her that Virgil admired. It seemed that he spent the biggest part of every day and every night worrying about his wife instead of working with her to find the end result in whatever they were striving towards.

The time they had spent getting to their mining spot seemed like a lifetime ago. The excitement they shared and revealing all of their most secret dreams to each other after they struck it rich had all been long forgotten. Now survival seemed to be the only quest they had at that point in time.

Finally Cassie had her feet on solid ground and Virgil was descending rapidly. Each one had a bag tied around them that they had placed their essentials in while they had been camping on the mountain. Home base was their wagon with a makeshift tent over the top of it not unlike a Conestoga wagon. They had been up the mountain for ten long days panning and digging and neither one of them had found so much as a tiny sparkle of gold to show for it.

"Mrs. Hollister are you ready to head to another dig site?" Virgil asked his wife.

"I am ready to hit this big gold strike you keep talking about Mr. Hollister," Cassie told him sounding a bit sarcastic.

"I know things ain't working out quite like I thought they would honey but we have to keep the faith. You ain't ready to give up yet are you? We spent every dime we had to get this far and I know there is gold here I can feel it in my bones," Virgil told her.

"I'll believe you when I feel it in my hand!" Cassie said sharply.

Virgil Hollister had always been a man with a great vision and that was one reason Cassie fell for him as they got older. He wasn't much on book smarts but he had a lot of common sense and Cassie had always been right to put her faith in him before.

"I'm sorry Virgil, you are right as always. I guess I am just still a little shook up from that climb down. I'll feel better after we get some hot vittles in our bellies and a good night's sleep," Cassie said and then she kissed his cheek.

"That's my girl!" Virgil replied as that flirty white smile crossed his lips and Cassie's heart fluttered once again.

Dinner was good and Cassie was ready for some well earned sleep when they heard a cry coming from the tree line.

"What in the world was that Virgil?" Cassie said sitting right straight up in the back of the wagon.

"I'm not sure honey, you want me to go check it out?" he asked.

Cassie nodded her head yes and Virgil pulled his trousers back on and slipped his wool coat on over his bare shoulders.

"I'll be right back," he told her as she handed him the rifle.

"You take this and be careful sweetheart," Cassie said concerned for his safety.

Virgil nodded that he would and carefully crawled out of the back of the wagon. He was gone what seemed like forever to Cassie but was actually only about fifteen minutes.

Cassie could hear footsteps coming close to their wagon and yelled out,

"Virgil, is that you?"

"Yes it's me Cassie, there is another campsite on the other side of the trees and a woman there just had a baby, poor thing," Virgil said as he stepped up into the wagon.

"A baby! Do you think I should go and see if she needs any help Virgil?" Cassie asked concerned for the new mother.

"Can you imagine giving birth in a place like this? Is there kin folk or someone there to help out Virgil?" Cassie asked.

"I saw quite a few folks over there and I'm sure she must be with her husband. What else would a woman be doing out here Cassie?" Virgil asked.

"You're right she must be with her husband. I hope they have enough supplies to take care of a baby and the mother. I think in the morning I will go to their camp and see if I can do anything for her. Is that all right with you?" Cassie asked.

The stars were shining brightly and Virgil saw the beautiful blue eyes of his loving wife and nodded yes.

The people had come in droves when in 1848 the first man found gold in California. Groups of ten to thirty men would join together in wagons and make the dangerous trek across the west to what they were told was the land of opportunity. At first the gold was an easy find but after 1849 it was harder to come by. The men suffered with disease from living in such filthy conditions and if that didn't kill them many of them starved or succumbed to the weather on their way to California. The only water supply was the river where they panned for gold and they cooked, bathed and used it as a toilet. Cholera was everywhere in the gold camps. Some men sank so low and deep into depression that they took their own lives. They had left their wives and children and spent all of their money to make the pilgrimage across the wild and unknown west. They thought going home with nothing would be too much of a disappointment to their families and they were ashamed to face them.

Morning came and after a hot pot of coffee and a biscuit or two Cassie and Virgil walked to the other side of the trees to meet the folks he had seen the night before.

There were tents and wagons scattered for quite a ways.

"Good morning friend," Virgil said to the first person he saw.

It was a little chubby man with glasses and thinning hair. He seemed to be deep in thought and was startled by the presence of the two strangers.

"We heard cries in the night and thought we would see if we could be of any service to your mining group here," Virgil said smiling at the little man.

"Good morning sir, we are not a gold mining group, well not so much anymore. We are homesteaders and wish to build a town and a place to lay down roots for our families," the chubby fellow said.

"What do you mean, "Not so much anymore", Virgil asked the stranger.

"Well sir, we started out from Boston to find gold and make our fortune but after living around this part of the country for over a year we have decided to stay and make it our home. We pulled in this area a couple of days ago after being threatened in San Francisco. There is a man there that has taken over the entire city and we are here to build a new city and make real jobs for ourselves and our families.

By the way, my name is Sam Noland, who might you be?" the fellow inquired.

"Oh, forgive me Mr. Noland, I am Virgil Hollister and this is my wife Cassie. We left Mississippi in hopes of finding a golden dream too," Virgil replied.

Virgil stretched out a hand to Mr. Noland and in turn his new friend did the same.

"You folks are kind of high up to start a town aren't you Sam?" Virgil asked.

"Oh we aren't starting one here son, we are just stopping for a while. One of the women here last night gave birth to her first child. We knew she would be coming into this world soon so we stopped to rest and let Rachel have her baby. She showed up a little sooner than we thought but we are blessed to have another person to join us," Sam said.

Virgil liked Sam right from the start and the two of them sat and talked while Cassie followed the sound of a crying baby.

The morning air was cool and crisp and Cassie looked at her surroundings. California was such a beautiful place and she could understand why the people wanted to dig roots here and make it their home. The mountainous area was filled with trees and other kinds of colorful foliage. Every so often Cassie would see a squirrel scurrying or a rabbit running for cover. They had seen plenty of deer and other wildlife since they had left the wagon train that they traveled with. Cassie had told Virgil that she thought Kansas was the most beautiful place she had ever seen with its never ending prairie and brilliant blue skies but she had changed her mind once she reached California.

Once again she heard the whimpering of a new born infant and Cassie hurried toward the sound.

"Hello," she said in a low tone.

"Hello," she heard coming from the inside of a wagon with a canvas top.

The material hanging down in the opening was pushed aside and there feeding the most precious baby Cassie had ever seen was the young mother.

"Pardon me, I am Cassie Hollister. My husband and I heard your baby crying last night and I wondered if there was anything I could do to help you Mrs.?" Cassie said letting her words wind down.

"I am Mrs. Bannister but please call me Rachel," the pretty fair haired lady replied.

"Hello Rachel is there anything I can do for you this glorious morning?" Cassie asked enamored by the sight of the tiny baby.

"Well, I believe little Annabel has had her fill if you wouldn't mind holding her while I button up I would appreciate that," Rachel stated.

"I would be delighted!" Cassie answered with enthusiasm as she took the tiny infant and cradled her in her arms.

Rachel buttoned up the front of her dress and said,

"You look real natural holding a baby Cassie do you have youngins' of your own?"

"Not yet but Virgil and me are wanting a large family someday. Hopefully we will find some gold soon so we'll have enough money to live in comfort and raise our children," Cassie replied with a widened smile.

Cassie and Rachel looked to be close in age and they hit it off right away.

"Where did you come from Cassie? Me and Will are from Missouri where we hooked up with the others," Rachel said.

"Virgil and me came from Jackson, Mississippi but we hooked up with a wagon train in Missouri as well," Cassie told her new friend.

Rachel took the baby from Cassie's arms and patted her back until the infant fell asleep. The sight of it made Cassie long for a child of her own. She put the thought out of her head and whispered to Rachel,

"I'll let you put her down and I will see you later."

Cassie quietly left the new mother to tend to her child and headed towards Virgil where he and Sam were talking up a storm.

"Did you get to meet the new youngin'?" Virgil asked his wife.

"Oh my yes and she is a pretty little thing. It was hard to give her back to her mama," Cassie replied with a bit of jealousy in her voice.

"Now don't you go getting any ideas Cassie we decided to wait until we have a proper home fit for raising kids before we start a family," Virgil reminded her.

Cassie nodded her head yes and dropped the subject. She felt an emptiness in her arms since giving Rachel her daughter back that she had never experienced before.

"I know you want to wait for a child Virgil but I think if Mrs. Bannister can handle a child out here so could we," Cassie told her husband with determination in her voice.

Virgil just shook his head and started walking towards the tree line on his way back to their base camp. Cassie could hear him mumbling to himself until he was out of her ear shot. She felt bad for what she had said knowing that the two of them had made a plan and had promised to stick to it. Cassie walked faster so she could catch up with her husband and apologize to him. The last thing she wanted was to make him feel bad. She knew in her heart that Virgil wanted a son or daughter as badly as she did but he was right in wanting to wait until they were settled. Cassie decided never to bring the subject up again.

Chapter 2

The morning began to warm as the sun peeked through the white and fluffy clouds. Virgil and Cassie were getting ready to climb the mountain again.

"This might be the day my dear," Virgil said trying to shift his wife's thoughts from Rachel's baby.

Cassie smiled at him as she tied her sack around her waist. She had filled it with the things she would need once they reached the summit. The two of them tied down the canvas on their wagon and headed for the foot of the mountain.

"You go first and I will be right behind you Cassie," Virgil said making sure he would be able to catch her in case she lost her footing.

Cassie nodded yes and started her uphill climb. Going up the mountain was a lot easier than climbing down. They had scaled the mountain so many times that they knew exactly where each foot should step heading up. Virgil had shoveled and picked steps to follow up but coming down it was hard to find the foot holds he had carved out for them. It was always much colder at the top and usually a week or so was all they were able to stand before they were exhausted and descended for some good sleep.

It would take them several hours of climbing to get to their camp site at the top of the mountain and it gave both of them time to think about what life would be like when they struck gold.

Cassie finally reached the top and as she pulled herself over the edge she quickly turned to make sure that her husband was close behind. Virgil was always right at her boot heels but this time he was not.

She called down to him,

"Virgil, is everything all right?"

"Yes," he hollered up to her.

"I found something on my way Cassie. It looks like a yellow streak through the rock. I think it may be a vein of gold!"

"Well don't tell the world," Cassie spouted as she started jumping around excitedly.

Virgil continued climbing until he was over the top of the ledge.

"I can't be sure but I think I may have found what we have been searching for Cassie," he told her with great anticipation.

"The only problem is that it is in a very difficult place to dig so we are going to have to come up with a plan where I can pick and send the rocks up to you," he told her.

The two of them put their thinking caps on and finally Virgil came up with an idea.

"If I take a long piece of rope and run it through a hole that I pick through that large rock over there then we should be able to run a bucket up and down the side of the mountain. That way the rock will make sure that the bucket is secure and won't fall after I fill it up. You can sift through the bucket and remove any gold nuggets," Virgil said.

"That sounds like a solid plan husband," Cassie replied so excited she could barely contain herself.

Cassie held the chisel as Virgil tapped away at the large flat rock that hung over the side of the ledge.

"Hold it still honey, I don't want to slip and hit your hand," he told his fidgety wife.

"I'm sorry Virgil I am just so excited I can barely keep from dancing a jig. We have worked so hard and finally this moment has come. We are going to be rich I can feel it in my bones!" Cassie said with jubilance in her voice.

"We don't know how much gold is in that streak if any and I don't want you to get your hopes up Cassie. I am going to break rocks and dig the ground out and if we find a strike then we can celebrate but for now let's wait and see what we find," Virgil told her calmly.

It took two days of tapping the rock with the stake to finally make a hole in it large enough for the rope to fit through and they both had a sore back.

"I think that will do Cassie. We have a hole large enough for the rope, go fetch it and I'll thread it through and tie the bucket on. I'll go back down the side of the mountain to where I found the yellow streak and we shall see how this works," Virgil told her.

Cassie was glad to finally stand upright and stretch her back. Bending over that rock for two days was not an easy task and Cassie could tell that Virgil was relieved that the job was done too.

She walked over to their camp site and found the rope and returned with it to Virgil.

"Here you go honey, I pray that after all that hammering this will work," she said glancing up at the heavens.

Virgil slipped the rope through the hole in the rock and then through the handle on the bucket. Then he tied the ends of the rope together so it was one large loop.

"Okay, I'm going down and when I get there you lower the bucket Cassie," Virgil told his wife.

Cassie stood on the edge of the cliff and watched as her husband carefully climbed down one careful step at a time. The mountain side where he had found the yellow streak was quite steep and not an easy place to dig. Cassie knew that one wrong move or a shift in the rocks could mean disaster for her man.

It took about twenty minutes for Virgil to reach his destination and Cassie let out a sigh of relief when he finally hollered up to her,

"Okay Cass, lower the bucket."

Cassie rolled up the rope in her hands and then gently pushed the bucket over the side of the cliff. Then she let the rope out slowly and the bucket descended perfectly down the side of the mountain.

"Is it there yet Virgil?" Cassie called down to him.

"Just a little more Cassie and that should do it," Virgil yelled back up to her.

Cassie let the rope down until she heard her husband holler,

"Whoa, right there is good."

Virgil picked up a few random rocks and scooped some dirt up in his hands and filled the bucket about half full. He knew that the weight would be a lot for his wife to pull up.

"Okay Cassie pull her up and let's see if this is going to work," Virgil said anxiously.

The bucket skimmed up the side of the mountain without a glitch and when it reached the top Cassie bent over and grabbed the bucket handle and pulled it over the edge.

"Got it!" Cassie exclaimed smiling at their ingenuity.

"I'm coming back up," Virgil yelled to her.

When Virgil finally climbed over the top of the ledge he put his arms around his wife and gave her a long and tight hug.

"Looks like this is gonna work!" he said smiling at her.

Virgil went over to the camp site and placed a burlap bag with a strap on it over his head and shoulder. He put a pick and the chisel inside. Cassie filled up a canteen of water and handed it to him and he tied it to his belt.

"Now when I yell up to you let the bucket down. It will be a while before I have broken through the rocks and there will be anything for you to pull up but once we get started it should go pretty fast. I won't make it so heavy that you can't pull it up," Virgil told Cassie.

Cassie nodded her head that she understood and knew that waiting for the first bucket of rock was going to seem like a lifetime.

"You be careful and don't take any risks," Cassie told him.

She reached up and kissed him on the cheek and watched as he started back down to where she hoped they would find their dreams.

"You let me know when you get there so I won't worry, okay?" Cassie asked.

"I will," he said as he started back down the mountain side.

Cassie sat on the rock waiting to hear from Virgil that he had reached the digging spot. Finally after about twenty minutes she heard him tell her that he was there.

"Well now," she said out loud to herself, "What am I going to do with this time I have on my hands?"

She began straightening up around the camp and getting prepared for another week or two on the mountain top.

Finally after a couple of hours Cassie heard Virgil calling her name and she raced over to the mountains edge.

"I'm here Virgil do you need me to lower the bucket?" Cassie asked.

"Yes send it down," he replied.

Cassie went about lowering the rope and bucket like they had rehearsed and when she heard Virgil holler she knew she had done her job.

After a short time she heard Virgil holler,

"Pull her up."

Cassie began pulling the rope and with it came, she hoped, a bucket full of dreams come true for the two of them.

"Got it!" she yelled down to Virgil.

She could hardly wait to start sifting through the bucket of dirt and rocks to see if there was anything shiny. First she pulled all of the rocks from the fill and then a little at a time poured the dirt into her sifting pan and sifted very carefully through it as to not over look anything. She found some gold dust in the bottom of the bucket and her hopes sky rocketed. She began hammering on the rocks trying to break them into smaller pieces and low and behold there it was a perfect gold nugget. It was not very large but it was indeed gold.

Cassie jumped up and down and leaned over the ledge and yelled down to her husband who was barely able to hold on as he picked and dug his way into the mountain side.

"Virgil, Virgil, you found it," she cried.

Virgil could hardly believe his ears as tears of joy ran down his cheeks.

"Yippee!" Virgil shouted as he found new energy with every swing of his pick.

"I knew it Cassie, I knew we would find gold," Virgil yelled back up to his happy bride.

"Lower the bucket honey and let me fill her up again," he shouted.

Cassie pushed the miracle pail back over the side and began reeling down the dream catcher to her husband.

Again and again Cassie found gold nuggets and gold dust in the bucket. They continued going on this way the entire day until finally Virgil knew he had to come up before dark or he would never be able to see the foot holds to climb the mountain.

"I'm coming up Cassie," Virgil called to his wife.

Virgil peeked his head over the top of the ledge and saw Cassie spinning in circles with her arms cradled as if she were holding an infant. His heart filled with love for her at the thought of her mothering his child. The sun was quickly sinking and the pink and orange colors in the sky as a backdrop made Cassie's dancing a vision to behold. Virgil looked up at the sky and thanked God for having such a full and happy heart.

Chapter 3

The next two weeks seemed to slip by very quickly and Cassie's bag of small gold nuggets was starting to fill. The two of them counted their blessings every morning and every night.

"We must have pretty near a half bag of gold Cassie," Virgil said as they sat around the camp fire eating dinner.

"Yes we do Virgil. What do you think it is worth?" Cassie asked as she day dreamed about all of her children dancing and playing in their large, happy home.

"I don't rightly know but it must be thousands of dollars," Virgil replied.

Neither of them had ever seen that much gold or had any idea of what it was worth. They assumed they were rich but the extent of their wealth was uncertain to either of them.

"I've been thinking that we should find a town and get the money for this gold Cassie. I don't want to take any chances of someone stealing it from us after all of the work we have done to get it. After we cash in we can come back and dig for more and we'll know how much money a bag of gold is worth. What do you think?" Virgil asked his wife.

"That sounds like fine thinking to me dear. We need more supplies anyway and maybe we can pick up a few things that we have had to do without," Cassie said smiling.

"What kind of things are you wanting Cass?" Virgil asked with a quizzical look on his face.

"Oh, just some pretty girl things and maybe a few new blankets and a couple of new lanterns. Nothing too foolish husband, I promise not to squander one dime on foolishness," Cassie said feeling a little selfish and ashamed.

"You buy anything you want Cassie, foolish or not. We can afford it now!" Virgil said as he stood up from the fire and raised a fist in the air.

The two of them began to laugh and Cassie rose up and they began to dance around the camp fire while Virgil sang a chorus of "Old Joe Clark".

The weather was changing up on the mountain and the north winds were making it almost impossible to hang on to the ledge and dig and pick without fear of falling. Winter was fast approaching and although it was still relatively warm down below it was freezing at the higher elevations.

"We'll pack up and head down tomorrow bright and early and make our way to town," Virgil said.

"Sounds good to me and I think we should check on Rachel and Annabel before we go in case they need anything," Cassie told her husband.

"That is a good idea we can see if anyone needs supplies from town Cass," Virgil said smiling.

Cassie raised the pot of coffee as she looked at Virgil and without saying a word he nodded his head no. She sat the pot on a rock away from the flames as Virgil threw an armful of branches into the camp fire. It was bedtime and it was cold. Cassie left all of her clothes on and crawled under the blankets of the bedroll which she shared with her loving husband.

"Come to bed Virgil and warm me up," Cassie said almost chattering her teeth.

"I'll be there in a moment Cass I want to have one more look at the gold before I go to bed," he answered.

Virgil took the bag of gold nuggets from its hiding place and carefully pulled the strings apart on top the pouch to reveal its contents. He could see the shiny stones as the light from the fire danced off of each golden rock. It was a sight to behold and he couldn't help but tear up thinking about all they had been through since they had left Mississippi. They had traveled through some terrible weather and had been attacked by Indians while the wagon trains rolled through central Kansas. Several of the men had lost their lives and their wives had been taken, screaming and kicking, horrified by their attackers.

"Was it all worth it Cass?" Virgil whispered as he stood looking at the golden nuggets in the pouch.

Cassie rolled over toward where her husband stood in the darkness.

"What do you mean Virgil? We came all of this way to find gold and we have found it. We had a dream back in Mississippi to become prospectors and strike it rich and my darling we have done it. Why would you even ask me that question?" Cassie asked troubled by his mood.

"I was thinking about the others on the wagon train, the men that were killed and the wives that were taken. I wonder what ever happened to those women. What if it had been you Cassie? What if I had been killed and the Indians had taken you?" Virgil asked while his voice became louder and shakier.

Cassie knew that he was not really asking a question but was being haunted by the Indian attack on the wagon train again. He had been having terrible nightmares about it ever since it had happened. He would wake up in the middle of the night screaming and crying out for help as he thrashed about under the covers.

Cassie rose from the bedroll and went to him. She encompassed him with her arms from behind and began to rock him back and forth.

"Why do you torture yourself over things that you have no power to change? I feel bad for those men and women too Virgil but we all took the same chance traveling through the west to find our fame and fortune. Some of them didn't make it but some of us did. Why can't you be happy for the people that did make it instead of wallowing in sorrow for those who did not?" Cassie asked him point blank.

"This cannot continue Virgil or you will surely go insane and then what will become of me?" she asked him trying to snap him out of it.

"You are right my dear, as usual. I don't know why this haunts me so. I try to put it out of my mind but for some reason I keep living it over and over again. I'm sorry, let's go to bed," Virgil told her as he turned towards her and enveloped her in his arms. He kissed her forehead and the two of them walked over to the bedroll. Virgil tied the bag of golden nuggets closed and placed it next to his side of the blankets.

They were both exhausted from all the work they had done and it didn't take long for the two of them to fall fast asleep. The fire made warm crackling sounds and the wind died down to being calm. Cassie rolled over on her back several hours later and gazed up into the heavens seeing a million stars.

The vastness of the universe had always enthralled Cassie.

Some nights, back in Mississippi, she would sit for hours staring into the starry night skies wondering about space and the creation of the universe.

Cassie had always been a woman of the brain where as Virgil was a man of the heart.

Finally she dozed back off to a dreamy, safe sleep until the sun rose over the edge of the earth. The brightness of the sun peeking over the mountain top was beautiful. There was a light coating of frost on the trees and the sun glistening on the leaves made them appear as if they were covered in tiny diamonds. The ground looked as though someone had covered it with a thin layer of icing.

"Wake up husband, we have a long day ahead of us," Cassie said as she gave Virgil's shoulder a shake.

"What, what are you doing?" Virgil replied still half asleep with his head buried under the blankets.

"It is a beautiful day and I don't want you to miss any part of it," Cassie announced as she pulled the warm covers from Virgil exposing his body to the cold elements.

"Oh!" he said as he raised straight up and pulled his trousers on as fast as he could.

"Are you making coffee you little menace?" Virgil asked grinning at his ornery bride.

"Just putting the pot over the fire now dear," Cassie answered.

"Just think Virgil, soon we will have a maid cooking for us and we can lounge in bed as long as we want," Cassie said with dreams of grandeur floating around in her head.

In a silly English accent Virgil looked at Cassie and as if tipping his hat and bowing said,

"Quite right my dear, quite right."

The two of them laughed and began chattering about their day sounding like a couple of excited squirrels. Cassie made some biscuits and found a jar of homemade blackberry jam.

"Yum," Virgil said after his first bite. "I declare Cass you make the best blackberry jam on either side of the Mississippi River girl. We could bottle that stuff up and sell it to kings in far away countries."

"Why thank you honey," Cassie said slightly blushing. She knew her jam and jelly was good but it was always wonderful to hear her husband brag about it.

Between the two of them they ate a whole pan of biscuits covered in blackberry jam and drank a half pot of coffee.

"It just can't get any better than that!" Virgil boasted as he wiped jam from his chin with his handkerchief.

They began packing utensils and rolling up bedding. Virgil kicked dirt into the flames until the camp fire was out and then stirred it with a wet branch to make sure there were not any hot embers left. The last thing he wanted to do was to start a fire on their mountain and destroy the beauty that was everywhere. Finally after a couple of hours they had all of their belongings packed up and were ready to start their descent down the mountain side.

Virgil took a piece of tablet writing paper and wrote:

This mountain is the property of Virgil and Cassie Hollister of Jackson, Mississippi.

We hereby stake a claim on October 22nd in the year 1850 on this site now called Mt. Blackberry.

Virgil took the paper and weaved it on a tree branch and stuck it in the ground.

"It is rightfully ours now Cassie. I can copy that paper and register it with any mining store and it will be all proper and legal," he told her.

Cassie clapped her hands together and then kissed her husband on the cheek like she always did before they started their downhill climb from the mountain. It was a dangerous task and just in case one of them fell to their death Cassie had decided that she would always kiss Virgil before they started down.

"Are you ready Mrs. Hollister?" Virgil asked her as he made his way to the mountain's edge.

"Yes Mr. Hollister I am ready," Cassie replied.

Virgil went first in case Cassie slipped. That way he might be able to catch her if she fell. The weather was colder than usual and Virgil felt that his joints were never going to oil themselves up enough for him to become more limber. Every step down was painful and it was hard for him to stretch out far enough to feel for the foot holds that he had dug. Sleeping on the hard and cold ground after hanging from the side of a mountain all day was a lot for anyone to endure.

Cassie had the bag of gold in her pouch tied to her waist and under her coat. If anyone was going to get it from her they would have to kill her first. She thought it would be smarter for her to carry it in case someone tried to steal it. They would never think that a young woman would be trusted with such a valuable load.

Carefully, Virgil started down the mountain side making sure that every step he took was the right one and telling Cassie which way to move first one foot and then the other so she would find the footholds. There were parts of the cliff that were full of rocks and tree branches that one could use for climbing but Virgil would not let Cassie put her weight on them unless he pulled or stepped on them first. He would not take any chances with her life no matter how much of a fuss she put up.

"You treat me like a little child Virgil Hollister," she would say after he scolded her several times for trying to step on a strange rock or ledge.

Cassie knew in her heart that he cared for her deeply and was only watching out for her safety.

She would always thank him for his thoughtfulness once they had reached the bottom of the mountain.

After several hours their trek had ended and finally they had reached solid ground. Cassie was ready to bend down and kiss the safe, flat ground after such a harrowing descent.

"We made it Virgil, let's get our wagon together now and head for the nearest mining town and see just how rich we are!" Cassie said exhausted.

"I'm going to cross the tree line and check on our neighbors and see if they need us to bring them back anything. You go ahead and start loading up the wagon. I hope the horse isn't dead," Virgil said under his breath.

Chapter 4

The horse was fine and Cassie was busy loading things up in the wagon when she heard Virgil screaming her name. The sound of his voice ran shivers up and down her spine. She thought for a moment that he was being attacked by a bear or a cougar the way he was wailing.

"I'm coming Virgil, I'm coming what's wrong?" Cassie cried out as she raced towards the tree line from where she heard her husband's voice.

As soon as she stepped into the camp site she knew what had happened. There were arrows sticking out from the wagons and death was everywhere. Cassie threw her hands over her mouth as she was afraid she may vomit from the grizzly sight. Virgil was standing in the middle of the camp shaking from head to toe with tears streaming down his wind burnt cheeks. There were their neighbors and new friends they had made lying dead all around them. Cassie walked over to Virgil and put her hand on his shoulder and said,

"This must have happened while we were up on the mountain. I wonder if there are any survivors."

"Annabel and Rachel!" Cassie screamed as she ran towards their wagon.

"Please God, not the baby," Cassie yelled until she finally reached the opening of Rachel's wagon.

Cassie could see red streaked blonde hair falling out of the partially opened canvas door of the wagon. She slowly walked up to her saying her name,

"Rachel, Rachel are you all right?"

Cassie peeked into the back of the wagon and saw that Rachel had several arrows in her chest and the top of her lovely blonde hair had been taken from her head. She shuttered and began to cry when she saw a blanket move.

Carefully Cassie took the edge of the blanket and pulled it up and there was Annabel looking at her not knowing that her mother was gone or that anything was wrong.

"Thank God!" Cassie said out loud as she picked up the baby and held her close.

"Your mama didn't make it Annabel but I will take care of you. You will know about your ma and how she must have hid you so the Indians wouldn't find you when you are older. I think we should leave this place now," Cassie whispered to Annabel as she carried the baby back to where Virgil was standing in shock.

Virgil felt a little better when he caught a glimpse of the baby that his wife was carrying.

"Rachel and the others are all gone but I found the baby hid under some blankets. Rachel must have put her there hoping that the Indians would not find her," Cassie told Virgil.

"Let's go Virgil, we need to take Annabel from this horrible place. We will raise her as our own and never tell her of this tragedy until she is grown. I think that is best don't you?" Cassie asked.

Virgil tried to get his wits back about him and analyze the situation. He looked around and saw that the Indians had pilfered the wagons before they left taking what they wanted.

"You go back to Rachel's wagon and see if you can find anything that Annabel will need, clothes, blankets or any baby items. I am going to see if I can find any bedding or food that will help us on our travels," Virgil told her.

"They would want to help us Cassie, especially since we have found little Annabel. Go on now and see if she has any baby clothes in the wagon," Virgil told his wife.

Cassie nodded yes and dashed back to the bloody scene keeping Annabel's head covered with the blanket she was wrapped in. Cassie didn't know if she could remember any of this since she was only a couple of weeks old but she didn't want to take any chances.

Cassie laid the baby down in her basket in the back of the wagon and began going through all of the clothes and supplies that were still there. She found some handmade gowns and crocheted booties that Rachel must have worked on while waiting for the birth of her child. They would mean a lot to Annabel when she grew up so Rachel checked through everything very thoroughly to make sure she had all of the baby's things. She came across a small deer skin bag and was relieved to know that she would have some way of feeding the baby once she figured out where the milk was going to come from.

Finally Cassie could no longer look at Rachel in that condition and placed a quilt over her body before she left. She said a prayer over the young woman and returned to her husband.

Virgil had found several bags of flour, sugar and three or four pounds of salted pork.

"I don't suppose there is a goat or a cow left around here is there Virgil?" Cassie asked looking at the baby in her arms.

"Why don't you take her and go back to our camp site and I will look around a bit more and see what I can find," Virgil told his shivering wife.

Cassie walked away not ever wanting to look back at the death and destruction that she had just seen. She prayed with every step she took that the wagon train of people had all found their way into heaven and that she would know how to be a good mother to Annabel. She couldn't help but think how happy they had been the night before, singing and dancing about on top of the mountain while all of these people were being massacred. The thought of it sent another shutter up her spine and she knew that dwelling on it would not help anything. She finally made it back to their camp and placed the basket inside of their wagon and pulled the canvas together to keep out the chill of the breeze. She finished up what she had started when she first heard Virgil calling out to her and before she knew it she had their wagon packed and ready to go. Although it was warmer where they had their base camp than it was on the mountain top it was still chilly and Cassie cradled Annabel in her arms and held her close to her for body heat.

Finally Virgil appeared through the tree line with several packs and bags slung over the back of a mule. Following the mule was a rope pulling a stubborn goat. The sight of the goat made Cassie smile.

"Here comes your dinner Annabel!" Cassie said as she rocked the baby back and forth in her arms.

She went to her wagon and retrieved the deer skin. It had been several hours since she had found the child and had no idea when her last meal had been so she knew that the baby needed to be fed right away.

Virgil knew this too so he found a pot and milked the goat and sat the pot over the hot embers of the fire for a few minutes before pouring the contents into the skin and handing it over to his wife.

"There you go mother," Virgil said as Cassie took the warm milk from his hand.

"I wonder how long it will take before I get use to being called mama." Cassie asked her husband.

"I think you'll do a right fine job of mothering that youngin' Cassie. You have wanted a baby for awhile now anyway," Virgil told her.

"Yes, but not this way. I know we will have other children but I promise that I will try to raise her and love her like she was yours and mine," Cassie said as she fed the hungry baby.

"Are we ready to head out?" Virgil asked his wife.

"Can we honestly leave all of those people scattered about without a proper burial Virgil?" Cassie asked.

"How can we come back here with all of this death so close to us? Think about the condition they will be in when we return," Cassie said.

Virgil knew she was right and he had all ready thought about the "condition of the bodies" when they returned. He needed his wife to tell him to make the right decision and bury those folks before they left. It would take several days or maybe even a week before he could dig enough graves for that many people but the situation would be even worse if they left them for several weeks.

"You mind staying for another week so I can get all of those fine folks in the ground proper like?" Virgil asked his wife.

"I think that is the decent thing to do Virgil," Cassie said.

"We will be fine here for another few days or a week unless..." Cassie's words faded as she thought.

"Unless what?" Virgil asked.

"Unless those Indians decide to come back. What if they are watching us now and decide to come back? We could end up like Rachel and the rest of them," Cassie said looking stunned and scared.

"I have to protect this baby Virgil, it is my duty as her mother," Cassie said starting to panic.

"Simmer down girl, why don't you and Annabel go ahead and leave if you are afraid. The wagon is all packed and I can catch up with you in a few days," Virgil told her.

"I can't leave you here all alone with such a horrible task to take on and I couldn't travel by myself with the baby for fear of another Indian raid," Cassie told Virgil.

"I don't know why they would return Cassie, they have taken all they want and left the entire community of people dead. You are letting your imagination run away with you. If you want to wait for me then wait but if you want to head out for Sacramento then head out. Whatever you decide will be fine with me," Virgil said.

"You have decided to go to Sacramento?" Cassie asked.

"I thought it would be closer than San Francisco and I hear tell that some man has taken over the entire town of San Francisco and charging people outlandish prices for anything they purchase there. Actually, it was the fellow from the camp across the tree line that told me that," Virgil said shaking his head.

"You are right as always Virgil. They have no reason to return and we are a family and we need to stay together. Anna and I will stay right here and I'll cook for you and help out any way I can," Cassie said glad of her decision.

"You called the baby Anna, is that what you want to call her? You know Cassie, you can name her anything you want to now," Virgil said quietly.

"Annabel is her name but I like Anna for short if that is all right with you, after all, you are her father now," Cassie said.

She watched the baby's eyes gently close as she fell asleep sucking on the now empty makeshift bottle.

"Isn't she the most precious thing you have ever seen?" Cassie asked Virgil in a whisper.

Virgil's eyes filled with tears as he witnessed his wife holding the new baby.

"Yes she is Cassie, she certainly is," Virgil whispered back.

Cassie took the sleeping baby over to their wagon and placed her in the basket and covered her.

"I might as well get this massive ordeal started Cass. I think there must be between twenty to twenty five people to bury. I should be able to take care of them all in three or four days. Then I am going to burn the wagons and dispose of any sign of them except for a marker I will erect later when we return from our trip to Sacramento," he stated.

"We need to give that place a name Virgil. I think we should call it something so it will be remembered. I also think that we need to tell some official in Sacramento what has happened here. Those people all had relatives who deserve to know what happened to their family members. I know we don't know all of them but we can give the names of the ones we did know. It may help someone someday," Cassie told Virgil.

He nodded his head yes and they both began to try and think up a good name for the community which he was about to bury for all time.

"What about Slaughterville or Massacre City?" Virgil said.

"Oh heavens no! It should be more of a spiritual name, I know, how about Heaven's Gate?" Cassie replied.

"I like it, okay Cassie, I am going to Heaven's Gate and start sending folks on their way," Virgil said as he tried to make this out to be more of a religious experience than a grueling one.

"When we get our money from the gold we will buy and erect a beautiful marker stating that this was a community called Heaven's Gate and that there was only one survivor named Annabel Bannister, daughter of Will and Rachel Bannister and put her birth date on it. It will be a tribute to all of the folks who lost their lives here," Cassie said as her mind drifted off to the marble marker she envisioned.

"Heaven's Gate right next to Mt. Blackberry sounds good to me Cass," Virgil said as he walked toward the tree line.

I'll unpack the cooking utensils and see what I can come up with for supper Virg. You are going to work up quite an appetite digging for three or four days," Cassie said as he finally was out of her sight.

Chapter 5

Annabel was quite a handful, something Cassie had never considered. The new mother had no experience raising a child on her own. Watching her younger siblings was an entirely different situation than this one. When her brothers or sisters became loud or hungry Cassie would go fetch her mother who was working in the fields or hanging laundry on a clothes line. Her ma would take over and Cassie would be on her way getting out of any real responsibility for the children.

This time there was no one else to fetch but Cassie was delighted to be a part of Anna's life and it didn't take long before she got the hang of it.

Three days had pasted and poor Virgil had blisters on his hands from digging so many graves for the folks at Heaven's Gate. He wanted to say a prayer over each one but decided due to the time it would take that he and Cassie would give one prayer for all when the last person was buried. He never considered this undertaking to be a burden and he felt very strongly that he was doing the proper and righteous thing. Cassie told him that he would most surely reap a great reward someday in heaven for this unselfish act.

At the end of the fourth day Virgil pounded his shovel on the dirt over the last grave. He was relieved to have finally finished and a spiritual mood came over him. He almost felt like a man of the cloth as he looked around at all of the fresh mounds of dirt. He made his way back across the tree line and told his wife that it was time to say a prayer over the dead. Cassie put a white shawl over her head and around her shoulders and lifted Anna from her basket.

They walked back to Heaven's Gate and when the Hollister's bowed their heads Cassie said,

"Lord, please look after these folks. They were good Christian people who were looking for a new home. I reckon they have found one with you now. Amen."

Virgil had scratched in a large rock the name of the town and the names of Will and Rachel Bannister along with that of Sam Noland. He had also put down Annabel Bannister as being the only survivor and the date of her birth like Cassie wanted.

"This will have to do until we return with our marker," Virgil said.

Cassie nodded that she approved and then Virgil looked at her and smiled and that was that.

There was no reason to stay and feel sorrowful so back to their camp they went. They packed up the last of their belongings in their wagon, hooked up their horse, tied the mule and goat to the back and headed for Sacramento.

They felt good and they felt blessed. The deer skin bag was working quite well as a means to feed the baby. Cassie would heat up a bit of milk from the goat and then pour it into the deer skin bag. She had cut away a tiny corner so the baby could suck the milk out without drowning herself. This was something that Cassie had seen her mother do when she could no longer produce milk herself for her own child.

The trip was rough and often Cassie was afraid that the jolt of the wagon wheels bouncing through holes and over jagged rocks would tear Anna completely from her loving arms. Virgil tried to drive the wagon more carefully with the addition of the baby but the terrain was mountainous and bumpy. There was no trail to follow and they realized that they may be the first people to cross this territory by wagon. There were no other ruts visible and they felt like a couple of explorers conquering a new frontier. It was an exciting adventure as they talked and pointed at different trees and birds. There was always something new to see and they loved every moment of the trip.

Off in the distance Cassie saw a large elk loping across a green field covered in yellow and white flowers.

"Isn't that about the prettiest thing you ever saw Virgil?" Cassie said as she pointed at the elk bounding across the meadow.

"Sure is Cass. I wish I had my gun up here, we could have eaten "pretty" well for quite awhile," Virgil replied.

Cassie slapped him playfully on the shoulder and they both laughed. The skies were a turquoise blue and every color of the trees, flowers and grass seemed to be more saturated than they had ever seen.

"Green is greener and blue is bluer here in California Cassie, don't you think?" Virgil asked.

"I know what you mean, it seems like God spilled more color here than he did in Mississippi," Cassie replied.

The time went by quickly and the family bond with Anna was growing stronger everyday for both Cassie and Virgil.

She was part of their family after only a week and Cassie and Virgil decided to call her Annabel Hollister in case anyone asked. They had all ready fallen in love with her and they didn't want anyone to be able to take her away from them like a blood relative of Rachel or Will's.

"We are her kin now Virgil and I don't see any harm in giving her our name. We can tell folks that I had her while we were mining our gold claim," Cassie said.

Virgil nodded giving his approval and nothing else was said about Anna's last name.

It took about ten days of hard going before the Hollister clan made it to the outskirts of Sacramento, California.

The town was new and fresh. The buildings had fresh paint and the wood and bricks were still all pristine. Cassie thought how lovely everything looked compared to the old and dirty city of Jackson Mississippi where she and Virgil had grown up.

The ladies walked along the board sidewalks dressed in beautiful clothing carrying parasols and the men had on suit jackets and derby hats. Some of the men even carried walking canes with silver or pearl handles, Cassie was quite impressed.

"Look at all of these fine people Anna," Cassie said to her daughter as they traveled through the streets of Sacramento for the first time.

"What a wonderful town Virgil. This might be a fine place to raise up a mess of youngins," Cassie said to her husband with a gleam in her eye.

"Don't you go getting any crazy ideas Cassie. We are here to cash in our gold and register our claim with the mining company. We are going to buy some new supplies and then we are going back and dig more gold out of Mt. Blackberry. Don't you remember our plan?" Virgil said with a bit of sarcasm in his voice.

"You are right Virgil as always, but it is still fun to dream about. I can see Anna now standing over there next to that white picket fence in her school dress waving good bye to me on her first day of school. She would be in a yellow polka dot dress with a bright yellow ribbon in her hair. She would be so pretty that all of the other little girls would just stay home from school," Cassie said laughing by the time she had ended her tall tale.

Virgil grinned like a crazy coon and shook his head.

"You can come up with some good ones Cassie, I'll sure give you that," Virgil said still grinning.

Cassie pointed down the street to the sign at announced itself as a mining company and they both began to get excited.

"This is it Virgil, now to see how rich we are. I hope we have room in this wagon for all of the money they are going to give us!" Cassie said smiling at her nervous husband.

"Let's wait and see what they offer us Cassie. I don't know what gold is going for anymore since the big boom a couple of years ago. We may not have enough to even buy supplies yet," Virgil said not wanting her to get her hopes up too high.

They didn't realize it but people were staring at them as their old horse pulled the makeshift wagon which led a mule and a skinny goat down the road. They had tried to keep themselves clean on Mt. Blackberry by washing in the river but it had been a long journey and they both looked fairly worn-torn from their travels.

Virgil pulled the wagon to a halt in front of the mining company and climbed down.

"I need the bag of gold Cassie," he whispered in a low voice.

Cassie reached inside of the wagon and pulled the bag out from under the blanket in Anna's basket. She had thought that would a safe hiding place. She handed it to Virgil and he started in the store carrying the gold in one hand and a life time full of dreams in the other.

"Don't forget to register our claim Virgil," Cassie yelled out to him.

He swatted his hand behind his back and she immediately quieted down.

Virgil tried to slick his hair down a bit upon entering the building and cleared his throat.

"Good afternoon, what may I do for you young man?" the fellow behind the counter asked Virgil.

"Good day to you sir. I would like to file a claim on a gold mine. I also have a bag here that I think you might be interested in," the young Hollister said.

"Well now, let's take a look at what you have," the clerk replied.

The balding, thin man shook the contents from the bag into a scale. He picked up one of the nuggets and gazed at it through some kind of a looking glass. All the while he was humming and hawing and Virgil was about to lose his mind.

"It looks like you have quite a find. There hasn't been many mine claims for quite some time. What did you say your name was son?" the clerk asked.

"Virgil, Virgil Hollister sir," he replied trying not to over react.

"My wife and daughter are out in the wagon would it be all right if I go fetch them?" Virgil asked like an excited school boy.

"Why yes indeed Mr. Hollister. I'm sure your family is anxious to find out what your gold is worth," the nice clerk replied.

Virgil raced to the doorway and motioned Cassie to come inside. She could see he was trying to contain his excitement and it made a warm and rosy feeling rise to her cheeks.

Cassie reached inside of the wagon and placed Anna it her basket. Then she hopped down and picked the basket up by its handles and started for the entrance to the mining company.

"What's the good news Virgil?" Cassie asked before she was in the doorway.

"I don't know yet, I wanted you to be here with me when I found out. You did your share of the work too Cass," Virgil said.

They walked back over to where the clerk was behind the counter and watched as he slid the weights back and forth. He was weighing the gold dust and the smaller nuggets on the scale and had the larger ones setting to one side of the counter.

He wrote down some numbers in a ledger and then he dumped the dust and nuggets back into the bag. He then placed all of the larger nuggets on the scale and went through his sliding ritual again. He picked up a gold rock and began scraping it with a tool that he pulled from a drawer and then put a few drops of some kind of chemical on the powder. Finally he put the larger nuggets back into the bag as well.

"Well Mr. Hollister, it looks like you have found yourself a nice gold mine. Your gold is not the purest that I have seen but it is gold and I believe that what you have brought in today is worth somewhere in the amount of one thousand dollars," the clerk said smiling at Virgil.

"Cassie looked somewhat upset and said,

"I thought it would be worth much more than that. We have worked so hard for that bag of gold Virgil."

"Do you know how long it would have taken us to make one thousand dollars in Jackson? We could have picked cotton or worked in the tobacco fields for years before we could have made half of that amount Cassie. Don't give up on me young lady, we have a lot more mining to do when we get back to Mt. Blackberry. Just remember honey, there is plenty more where that came from," Virgil told her.

"You are right, as usual husband and one thousand dollars is a lot of money. I'm sorry Virgil, I just wanted to hit it big and go home I suppose. I know our dream is something we will have to work for. Where do we register our claim Mr.?" Cassie asked the mining clerk.

"My name is Roy Simon and I will be happy to file your claim for you," the mining clerk conveyed.

Mr. Simon retrieved several forms from a drawer and began asking Virgil questions about the location of their gold mine. It took about thirty minutes to get everything down that the clerk wanted.

"We have to be very careful and very specific with our claims now Mr. Hollister. There are claim jumpers everywhere and without the proper registration someone could just take your mine away from you. You can be sure that Mt. Blackberry and Heaven's Gate now have a legally registered deed and both properties are in your name," Mr. Simon told them.

"We own Heaven' Gate Virgil?" Cassie asked in amazement.

"It is the only way I could establish it as a real community Cassie. I told him that about twenty five people resided there," Virgil said in a low voice as he raised his eyebrows up and down.

Cassie understood and said no more about Heaven's Gate in front of Mr. Simon. Virgil put his signature on the deeds and the mining clerk stamped and filed them in a long cabinet.

"Now for your money Mr. Hollister," the clerk said.

He opened a safe and counted out one thousand dollars on the counter to Virgil and Cassie.

"I suggest you get most of this in a bank if you want to keep it," Roy told them.

Cassie and Virgil had never seen that much money before.

Chapter 6

Virgil folded the large wad of money and stuffed it inside his boot.

"He's right Cass, we can't take no chances with all of this money. What do you reckon we should do with it?" Virgil asked his wife.

Cassie thought for a moment and then said,

"Well we don't want to leave it here if we are going back to Mt. Blackberry. It took a long time to reach Sacramento and what if we decide to head home or somewhere else after we mine more gold? I think we should think of a real good hiding place Virgil and take it with us."

Virgil shook his head yes and the two of them left the mining company a fairly wealthy couple. They headed straight for the general store to buy supplies and then to a clothing store to buy new britches and shirts for Virgil. Cassie found a lovely dress with a pattern of blue flowers on it and Virgil had her try it on.

"You look like a dream Cassie. You must let me buy you that dress," Virgil told her with that smile of his gleaming.

"Why do I need a new dress when I am camping in the mountains and mining for gold Virgil Hollister?" Cassie replied in a scolding tone.

"Won't you let me spoil you a little Cassie?" Virgil asked his sensible wife.

"We have all of this money and we've always had to scrimp for everything we wanted. I know it seems odd to be able to go in and buy whatever we please but let's do it. We are going back to mine more gold, let's have some fun Mrs. Hollister, we deserve it," Virgil said.

"You are right as always Virgil but remember we need to buy a marker of some kind for Heaven's Gate," Mrs. Hollister replied.

Cassie let her guard down about the money and they spent over an hour buying new duds, supplies and lots of baby things.

Every time Cassie would see something different for Annabel she would throw her hands up and say, "Oh my how precious," and Virgil would put it on the counter with the other items they were going to purchase.

They bought food and blankets and mining supplies. New hats, coats, lanterns and coal oil made the list too.

"I think we need to go to the livery stable and see about a new horse and wagon Cassie. The one we are traveling in is about to fall apart. What do you think my dear?" Virgil asked his wife.

Cassie was happy to get rid of the old rickety wagon and into a new solid one. She had never really formed any kind of a bond with their horse and he was old and worn out when they bought him. He had brought them all of the way from Mississippi and how he had managed to travel so far at his age was still a mystery to Cassie.

"You know Virgil, that old horse has a lot of heart," Cassie said thinking about all of the miles he had traveled.

"I hope his last days are good ones," she said.

Virgil took the money from his boot and paid the clerk and gathered up their supplies. They stepped out onto the boardwalk and headed back to their horse and wagon.

Cassie couldn't help but stop and rub the old horse on the nose before she stepped up and took a seat.

Virgil put the supplies in the back of the old wagon. The livery stable was just down the road and Virgil took the horse by the halter and led him to the stable.

Cassie rocked Anna back and forth in her arms to the clip clop of the horse hooves. She began singing a little song to her and before they reached the stables Annabel was fast asleep.

"I'll put her back in her basket and then we can take a look at the horse stock for sale," Cassie told Virgil.

Virgil helped Cassie down with the baby basket and they walked into the livery stable together.

"Howdy folks what can I help you with?" asked the stable man.

"We are looking to trade in our horse and wagon for a new set up mister," Virgil told the muscular livery man.

"What kind of wagon are you looking for son," the stable man asked.

"My wife and I need something that is solid and dependable. We are traveling over some rocky terrain and I want to make sure that we arrive safely," Virgil said trying to sound like a man of the world.

"Let's take a look at what you have now and see what we can trade it for," the man said.

"No, no you don't understand sir, I have the money to pay for a new wagon and a young strong horse. I just don't have the need to keep what I have now so I would like for you to take it as part of the deal," young Hollister told the stable man.

"The name is Henry son what is yours?" the livery man asked.

"My name is Virgil Hollister and this is my wife Cassie and our daughter Anna," Virgil said as he smiled at the big man.

They all walked back out of the livery stable and Henry took a look at what Virgil wanted to trade. Henry shook his head and tried not to laugh out loud.

"The goat will go with us but the mule, wagon and horse are yours," Virgil told him with a serious face.

Henry could see that Virgil was trying to make a deal with him and so he shook off the urge to laugh and said,

"I'll give you ten dollars for all of it except the goat."

Virgil looked at Cassie and said,

"What do you think honey?"

"I think you are trying to swindle us sir. Why our horse is worth more than ten dollars and I know this mule must be worth at least ten or fifteen and that isn't even counting the wagon. We may not be city folk but we ain't stupid folk either," Cassie told Henry point blank.

Henry thought for a moment and decided that in the event that they did have the money for a horse and wagon he didn't want to rile them so he apologized and made an offer of thirty dollars instead.

Virgil looked at Cassie and she nodded yes and Virgil and Henry shook hands. Henry took thirty dollars out of his pocket and handed it to Mr. Hollister which in turn handed it to Cassie.

"Let's go see what we can get for you Virgil," Henry said as the three of them walked back into the stable.

While Henry was showing Virgil several different wagons Cassie was captivated by the sight of a beautiful white horse in the stalls. The animal reminded her of something that a princess would ride with a long flowing mane and tail. The horse seemed to be high spirited and had beautiful muscular lines. Cassie walked over to the stall and spoke very softly to the handsome horse.

"Hi girl my name is Cassie, what's yours?" Cassie asked as if the horse would answer her back.

"We call her Spirit," a soft female voice said.

Cassie spun around and saw a pretty young girl approaching her.

"Hi, I'm Nellie I didn't' mean to startle you ma'am," the young girl said.

"You didn't, my name is Cassie, is this your horse?" Cassie asked still staring at Spirit.

"No she is not ours but she does belong to someone here in Sacramento. We are boarding her for a few days while the owner is out of town. Isn't she stunning?" the young girl asked not needing an answer.

"Do you think the owner would be willing to sell her Nellie?" Cassie asked.

"I don't know you would have to ask him," Nellie replied.

In the meantime Virgil had made a deal with Henry about a wagon and they had started towards the stables in search of a horse or two to pull it.

"Virgil," Cassie yelled. "Come over here and look at this amazing horse."

Virgil stepped away from Henry and approached Cassie seeing the white beauty while still walking towards her.

"What a magnificent horse!" Virgil said in a loud voice.

"I sure would like to buy her. The owner is out of town for a few days. Her name is Spirit and I think she is the most beautiful horse I have ever seen," Cassie said sounding childlike.

"If you want her then we should wait for the owner to come back to town and see if he would be interested in selling her Cassie," Virgil told his wife happy to see such a smile on her face.

"It is all coming together Virg, I have you, Annabel the gold mine and now if I can have Spirit we will be one happy family," Cassie said barely able to hold her composure.

"She sure is a looker. Could I go in the stall and check her out Miss?" Virgil asked the young girl.

"Her name is Nellie," Cassie replied.

Virgil tipped his hat and said, "Nice to meet you Nellie."

"I don't see any harm in it. She is a little high spirited so stay calm until she gets use to you," Nellie warned Virgil.

The young girl opened the gate to the stall and Virgil slipped through holding out a hand to the skittish white horse. He walked closer to her with his hand out and soon he had it right under her nose. Spirit rubbed his hand and then Virgil began stroking her velvet nose and talking calmly to her.

"There now girl I won't hurt you," he said as he began running the palm of his hand down her long silky face.

Her lines were exquisite and her mane and tail were long and flowing down her neck and hind quarters.

"If she had a horn coming from her head she would look like a unicorn," Virgil said as he stroked her mane and patted her long massive neck.

"I bet the owner would want a fortune for her," Cassie said as she dreamed about riding Spirit through a meadow bareback.

"Well if he will sell her she will be ours. I told you Cassie, money ain't no good unless you get what you want with it," Virgil told his wife.

"Is there a hotel close by?" Cassie asked the young girl.

"Yes, just around the corner and down the road a bit," Nellie replied.

"If you want to stay and meet the owner of this horse I will make sure that he knows about you when he arrives back in town. I can tell him where you are staying so you can talk business with him," Nellie told Virgil.

"That would be just fine Nellie. Thank you and now I have a new wagon to load so Cassie if you and Anna want to go check into the hotel I'll unhitch our horse and move our belongings into our new residence," Virgil said with a smile.

"I traded the old wagon and the horse and mule besides some money. I guess I should have made sure that was all right with you first honey. You want to come and see what I picked out?" Virgil asked his wife.

Cassie had to tear her eyes away from the white horse but finally nodded yes and followed her husband to the back of the stables. There was a new wagon made of hardwood with a nice weather top on it. It was twice the size of their old wagon so there would be plenty of room for the three of them to sleep and pack their supplies in.

"Oh Virgil this is wonderful!" Cassie gasped.

"Which horses have you purchased to pull it?" she asked.

"Well I thought you wanted that white horse? Isn't that why we are staying to see if we can buy her from the owner?" he asked.

"Yes I want her but she is not a wagon horse, she will be a riding horse. I could never put a harness on such a beautiful creature. You need to find a couple of young horses to pull the wagon Virgil," Cassie told her husband.

Virgil just shrugged his shoulders and motioned the stable man over to where the other horses were stalled.

"Any of these horses for sale Henry? I guess the wife wants me to buy a couple of young horses to pull the new wagon," Virgil told him.

Henry pointed out several horses to young Mr. Hollister and the horse bartering began. After about twenty minutes Virgil and Henry had come to a mutual agreement and Virgil pulled more money out of his boot and paid the stable man for the two horses.

In the meantime Nellie took Cassie and Anna to the hotel and helped her get checked in.

"Mr. Stern is the desk clerk's name and he is a real nice man so if you need anything just ask him and he will be happy to help you out Cassie," Nellie told her new friend as she walked out of the hotel lobby and headed back toward the stables.

Mr. Stern handed Cassie a room key and told her which room was hers.

"You and your family will be in room seven Mrs. Hollister."

The hotel was quite grand and Cassie had never been in an establishment of that quality. The drapes were gold and green and were hanging down to the floor. There was a huge marble table in the center of the lobby with a large vase of fresh cut flowers in it. The wallpaper had green checks of velvet running in vertical rows the length of the wall. Cassie was excited to see what their room would look like. She hurried up the winding staircase carrying Annabel in her arms until she found a room on the second floor with a number seven on the door.

"This must be it Anna," she said whispering to the baby in her arms.

Cassie unlocked the door with the key the clerk had given her and was astounded by what she saw upon entering.

The room was majestic in every way. There before her was the largest bed Cassie had ever seen with a beautiful canopy over the top of it. The furniture was a shiny maple and was very large and bulky. Everything in the room was accented with the color blue. There were blue velvet drapes in the windows and a blue spread across the bed.

"So this is what it's like to have money," Cassie said out loud in a low voice.

Chapter 7

Annabel was getting sleepy and fussy so Cassie laid her down in the middle of the overstuffed bed. She lay down beside her and loved how the feather mattress enveloped her body. This was the most comfortable bed she had ever been on and she knew right away that someday Virgil would have to buy her one for their new home. It only took a few minutes and the two of them were sound asleep.

An hour or so had passed and Cassie was awakened by a gentle rap on the door. It took her a moment to realize where she was and then she sprang from the bed and asked quietly at the door,

"Who is it?"

"It's me Cass, let me in," Virgil replied.

Cassie unlocked and opened the door for her husband.

"I have the new wagon loaded with our things and our supplies. I left the two horses I bought in the stables until we are ready to leave. Henry said we could leave them there all week if we wanted and he would feed and water them for free. I really like the folks in Sacramento don't you Cass?" Virgil asked.

"Yes, yes I do Virgil. What do you think of this place? Did you see the lobby and just look at this bed and this room Virgil!" Cassie said talking faster than usual.

"I'm going to like having money and all of the things that come with it," Cassie said smiling as she gazed at their expensive surroundings.

Her husband smiled at her then kicked off his boots and tried out the soft mattress.

"This is the softest bed I have ever been on honey," he told his wife.

"I know, I thought the same thing. Someday when we get our house I want a bed just like this one with the canopy on top," Cassie said.

The twinkle in her eye told Virgil that she was warming up to the idea of having nice things that only money could buy.

"I'm going to take a bath, would you watch Anna while I am in the bath room?" Cassie asked her husband.

"She is sound asleep so I'm just going to lay here beside her and take a nap," Virgil told her.

Cassie took her new dress and other personal garments and left the room in search of a nice warm soak.

It didn't take Virgil long to drift off to sleep and begin dreaming about a fine home full of children. An hour or so later Cassie came back to the room looking very pretty in her new dress with her hair shiny and clean.

She shook his shoulder to wake him up and said,

"Okay my dear it is your turn. I want you to go take a bath and put on some clean clothes. You are not about to get under these fine linens next to me smelling like an old goat."

Virgil tickled her side and she began to giggle and Anna woke from her nap.

"Now look what you have done, you woke up the baby," Cassie said teasingly.

"Okay, let me get my new duds and I'll take a bath. That sounds real nice anyway," Virgil replied grinning at her.

It didn't take him long to leave so Cassie took Annabel downstairs and asked Mr. Stern if he had a bottle of milk so she could feed the baby. The desk clerk looked at her a little puzzled and then said he would see what he could find.

"I guess it does seem strange that a new mother would need to feed her new baby with a bottle," Cassie whispered to Annabel.

"Oh well, it is none of his business anyway," she continued.

A few minutes passed then Mr. Stern came back with a bottle of milk and Cassie asked him to charge it to their bill and he nodded his approval.

After Virgil returned to the room all clean and shaven the three of them went out to find a nice place to have their dinner. For the first time in her life Cassie was going to eat at a fine restaurant. She had never been so pampered before and loved the treatment.

Several days came and went and every day the three of them would walk along the board walk and look in the windows of the stores. Sometimes one of them would get excited and they would have to go inside and purchase the article they had seen in the window.

On the third morning as they were getting ready to go out for their daily stroll someone knocked on their hotel door.

"Yes, who is it?" Cassie asked.

"Good day ma'am, I am Billy Ashton, I own the white mare in the stables. The young girl Nellie told me that you were interested in buying her," the voice on the other side of the door replied.

Cassie hurried to open the door and greet the owner of what she hoped would soon be her horse.

As the door opened Cassie was startled to see a man standing there in shabby clothes who appeared to be as poor as they had been before they found the gold.

Oh, good morning Mr. Ashton," Cassie said embarrassed at how she must have looked when she first laid eyes on him.

"I guess I'm not what you were expecting ma'am," Mr. Ashton said looking down at his dirty and torn clothes.

"I have been out of town and have not had time to clean up. I came as soon as I heard you were interested in purchasing Spirit," Mr. Ashton told her.

"Please forgive me sir, I didn't mean to embarrass you. I apologize for my behavior," Cassie said looking ashamed.

"Nonsense my child, I understand perfectly. You were expecting to see a business man dressed in fine clothes and instead you see before you a dirty saddle tramp," Mr. Ashton said smiling.

"Oh no, sir," Cassie said.

"Let us just forget first impressions my dear and get down to the business at hand, my horse Spirit," he said smiling at her.

Cassie smiled back and invited him into their room.

"Mr. Ashton this is my husband Virgil Hollister and I am his wife Cassie. We happened upon your horse while we were purchasing a new wagon and a team. She is a beautiful mare and I fell in love with her at first sight. Are you interested in selling her?" Cassie asked with high hopes.

Virgil reached out to shake hands with Mr. Ashton and the two of them said their hellos to each other.

"I must admit that I am rather surprised at your ages," Ashton said.

"I was expecting an older couple. You can see that my mare is quite an expensive horse so I just assumed that the couple interested in purchasing her would be, shall we say, a little more mature in their net worth," Ashton stated.

"Oh we have a very good net worth Mr. Ashton.

"Cassie please," Virgil said giving her an unhappy look.

"Why don't you and Anna go down to the lobby and let me and Mr. Ashton talk business," Virgil said raising an eyebrow at her.

Cassie felt uncomfortable all of a sudden and picked up Anna and left the room.

"So you are one of the lucky chaps that have discovered a gold mine," Ashton said.

"Oh no we just found a small pouch of gold dust Mr. Ashton, not anything to get excited over. You will have to forgive my wife she is not use to having any money and well, she sometimes over exaggerates our monetary value," Virgil said trying to undo what Cassie had told this perfect stranger.

"Don't worry young man your secret is safe with me," Ashton replied.

"Are you interested in selling the horse?" Virgil asked him point blank.

"I couldn't possibly sell her for anything less than two hundred dollars," he answered.

"That is a lot of money for one horse sir," Virgil said alarmed at the price.

"If you knew anything about horses young man you would know that Spirit is quite a specimen and that a horse like her is rare in these parts. I acquired her not long ago so I have not made any real bond with the horse yet. I have been gone for over a week and plan on leaving town again soon on business. She could use a good home and someone to spend time with her. I don't know if she is even saddle broke," Mr. Ashton told Virgil.

"Let me talk it over with my wife and we will get in touch with you by tomorrow morning. We plan on leaving town then. Where can we find you with our answer?" Virgil asked.

"Oh, I'll be at the stables first thing in the morning Mr. Hollister. I'll see you then," Ashton answered.

The two men shook hands again and he let himself out of the hotel room.

Cassie and Anna were looking through some books in the lobby and saw Mr. Ashton tip his dirty torn hat at them as he left the hotel.

Cassie raced up the stairs and saw Virgil standing in the open doorway of their room.

"What did he say Virg, is he willing to sell her?" Cassie asked barely able to contain her excitement.

"Yes he will sell her Cass but he wants two hundred dollars for her. That is a lot of money for one horse," Virgil told his wife.

"I don't know why but I have a funny feeling about him Cassie. I don't trust him. I don't think he is what he appears to be. Whether he has been traveling or not why would he show up looking like a tramp?" Virgil said shaking his head.

"We can afford two hundred dollars Virgil, I'll take back all of the other things I have bought since we have been here if you let me buy the horse," Cassie said anxiously.

"I don't know Cass, something just doesn't feel right. I know you have your heart set on getting Spirit but I think we should tell him we have changed our minds and get back to the gold mine," Virgil told his wife.

Cassie was heartbroken but she knew that Virgil was usually right about his feelings and if he felt uneasy about the deal then she would try and let it go.

"Whatever you say Virgil, I'll go along with whatever you say," Cassie said in a low voice.

"Once we mine more gold and get back to Mississippi I'll buy you a whole herd of white horses honey," Virgil said putting his arms around her and Anna.

"Okay," Cassie said trying to conjure up a little smile for her sympathetic husband.

"I'm going to go take care of some last minute purchases we need before we head out tomorrow Cassie. Is there anything I can get you dear?" Virgil asked his disappointed wife.

"No, I have everything I need for Annabel. I think we will be fine," Cassie told him.

Virgil kissed her cheek and left the hotel.

On his way to the general store Virgil saw Mr. Ashton talking to another man standing next to the saloon. He was just as dirty and tattered as Ashton and Virgil had an unexpected chill run down his spine.

He made a stop at the gunsmith shop and purchased a six shooter and several boxes of bullets.

Virgil slipped the gun in his belt under his jacket and headed on down to the general store. After he made a few purchases there he stopped by the livery stable and asked Henry if he owed him any more money.

"Did you buy the mare?" Henry asked.

"No, I don't think we are going to pay that price for her. She is a beauty but for two hundred dollars I can buy three just like her back home," Virgil told the stable man.

"Henry, Mr. Ashton is going to be here in the morning to find out my decision on the horse. Would you please let him know that we have decided not to buy her? I think we are heading out today," Virgil said.

"You don't owe me a dime Mr. Hollister and I'd be happy to let him know your decision on the mare. It was nice to meet you folks and thanks for your business," Henry told Virgil as the two men shook hands.

Virgil started out of the door and then stopped and turned to Henry and asked,

"Do you know anything about Billy Ashton?"

"No I am afraid I don't. He brought the mare in a couple of weeks ago. He has never paid his bill on her. I wondered how a man like him came to have such a beautiful horse but it isn't really my business," Henry replied.

Virgil shook his head yes as if to agree with him and then hurried back to the hotel to tell Cassie that they were leaving town.

"Why are you in such a hurry Virgil? I thought we were going to leave after we spoke to Mr. Ashton," Cassie asked confused.

"Henry is going to tell him and I just want to get back to work Cassie. The sooner we get back to Mt. Blackberry the sooner we can start digging again," Virgil told her.

Cassie started mumbling to herself but began getting all of her and Anna's things together. She put them in a red flowered satchel that she had bought at one of the town's finer shops.

While she was busy packing Virgil had the horses hitched to the new wagon and had it waiting out front of the hotel for them. He went back to the room to see if Cassie and Annabel were ready to pull out.

"Okay dear, we are as ready as we'll ever be," Cassie said to her husband.

Virgil picked up the satchel, went down the stairs and only stopped in the lobby long enough to pay the bill. The two of them climbed up on the new wagon and with Annabel in her arms Cassie waved at Henry as they rolled out of Sacramento.

"I forgot to tell you Cassie that I had a plaque made for Heaven's Gate. I picked it up and loaded it in the wagon this morning while you were packing. It isn't a large plaque but it is a good one and will withstand all kinds of weather," Virgil said.

Cassie squeezed his arm and smiled at him saying,

"You are such a good man, I am truly blessed to have you in my life Virgil Hollister."

The wagon ride was smooth and the horses were quick steppers as the Hollister's headed back to Mt. Blackberry.

Chapter 8

The morning was a dandy one with wisps of white clouds floating across a blue sky. The warm sun was bright and shining on them as they rode further and further away from civilization.

"I put the goat in the back of the wagon," Virgil told Cass.

"I didn't want to walk her to death on these rocky roads," he said.

"Good idea husband," Cassie said as she enjoyed the scenery as they traveled.

She didn't know it but Virgil was being very wary of their surroundings. He was always looking just a little further up the road to make sure that no one was ahead waiting to ambush them.

"Why are you so tense dear?" Cassie finally asked him.

"You keep looking ahead and then behind are you worried about something?" she asked her husband.

"No, just looking at this beautiful countryside," Virgil said not wanting to upset his wife.

The days came and went without a hitch and they both loved their new wagon and horse team. Cassie would go inside the wagon and put Anna down in her new wooden crib full of fluffy blankets for her nap. She had bought some yarn and had knitted her a new hat. Sometimes she would sit inside the wagon out of the sun and knit while Anna was asleep and sometimes she would sit up front with Virgil and they would talk for hours about how happy their lives were going to be.

"We should reach Mt. Blackberry by tomorrow Cassie. I think we should come up with a new plan. I don't know how you are going to scale the mountain with Anna," Virgil said concerned for his family.

"I have been thinking on that too Virg. I have been knitting a bag with straps on it to put her in while I climb up. I can put it on my back much like a papoose that the Indians use," Cassie replied.

"Pack her on your back huh, that is a good idea. Of course a better idea is that you stay below while I climb up and mine the gold," Virgil said in a louder tone.

"Now you listen to me Virgil Hollister, we got into this together and we will continue together. Just because we now have Annabel doesn't mean that I am going to sit at the base camp all day while you do all of the work. I think my papoose idea is a good one. I will try it out on level ground before I try going up the side of the mountain," Cassie told him determined.

Virgil knew his wife well enough to nod and let her have her own way. He had learned a long time ago that once Cassie got something into her head that she was not likely to change her mind until she at least tried it.

Cassie knew her husband too, and knew that he would let her have her own way when she became stubborn enough.

She reached over and gave him a quick kiss on the cheek and said, "Now that is settled where do you suggest we set up camp tonight?"

"If we keep on going we can be there in a few hours but this trail is so rocky that I don't think we should chance hitting a rock or hole in the dark and breaking our new rig. Besides, some of these cliffs are pretty treacherous and I am not taking any chances when it comes to you and Anna," Virgil told her.

"I think around the next bend is a stand of oak trees and that would be a good place to stop for the night. We can get an early start at sun up and be at Mt. Blackberry fairly early tomorrow morning. Does that sound alright with you dear?" Virgil asked.

"That sounds fine with me. I need to get out of this wagon and stretch my back and legs. I have been bounced up and down until I am worn out husband," Cassie said bobbing her head up and down giving him a visual effect.

"Oh Cassie," Virgil said laughing out loud at her antics.

The tree row was right where Virgil remembered it and Cassie had baby Anna in her arms and was ready to climb down from the wagon when he yelled. "Whoa!" and put on the brake.

She handed Anna to her husband and climbed down and then reached up for him to hand Anna back to her. It felt wonderful to walk around on solid ground and get the kinks out of her back and legs.

"You take a walk Cassie, I'll get some wood gathered for a fire. The sun will be down soon and I don't like being out here with the baby in the dark," Virgil said.

Cassie and Anna walked into the tree line and looked at all there was to see. The leaves were turning a gold and orange color that Cassie had never seen before. Some of them had already fallen and made a crunching sound under her feet. Red squirrels were dashing everywhere with their bushy tails jerking one way and then the other.

Virgil gathered dead branches and limbs that had fallen from the trees.

"This dried oak will make a warm and roaring fire Cassie," Virgil yelled out not seeing them in his sights.

"Cassie, you hear me darlin'," Virgil yelled out again.

There was silence except for the scurrying of the squirrels on the downed leaves.

"Cassie, Cassie!" Virgil cried out as he headed for the place he had seen his wife and child enter the tree line.

At that instant Virgil saw the white mare come walking out from behind a giant oak tree. It was the same mare they had wanted to purchase and riding her was none other than Billy Ashton.

"Ashton, what are you doing out here?" the startled Virgil asked abruptly.

"How do Mr. Hollister. I was wondering the same about you. We must be close to your gold mine are we not?" Ashton said in a low tone with a strange smile on his face.

"I, I don't know what you are talking about Mr. Ashton," Virgil answered.

"I am looking for my wife and child. They came into the tree line here. Have you seen them?" Virgil asked with a shaky voice.

"Why yes as a matter of fact I have seen them Hollister. I'll be happy to take you to them...as soon as you take me to your gold mine!" Ashton shouted at him.

Virgil forgot all about being scared and took a run toward his nemesis. Ashton drew a six shooter from his holster and shouted,

"You better hold it right there boy if you ever want to see your wife and daughter again. Now you take me to your gold mine. Me and the boys are going to take over your claim," Billy said grinning ear to ear.

Virgil stopped dead in his tracks and asked,

"What makes you think I have found a gold mine Mr. Ashton?"

"Well let me see boy, a couple of strangers come into town in a broken down wagon looking poor and shabby. They stop by the mining company and come out buying clothes and new horses and a new wagon. What do you take me for son, a darn fool? I saw you pulling money from your sock. You kids should have been a little more careful the way you were spending money all over town," Ashton told Virgil pointing a gun at his head.

"I thought you were out of town, how could you have known what we were doing?" the young Hollister asked him.

"I've been around and so have my boys. You see son that is our line of business. We see who comes in town with nothing and leaves with a lot. That way we know who has a producing mine and then we follow them and they take us right to it. It's as easy as that," Billy told him.

"So help me God if you hurt my family you will pay with your life!" Virgil yelled out to Ashton.

"Nobody has to get hurt here Virgil. You just lead us to the mine and we will return your wife and baby," Ashton replied.

"It is still a few hours away. We were only bedding down here for the night and then going on in the morning. The path is, too rocky to drive a wagon through here after dark," Virgil told him feeling beaten.

"Okay we will bed down here for the night and then at first light we go to the gold mine," Ashton said.

"Come on out boys and see if this young man is toting a gun," Ashton called out to his band of crooks.

"What about my wife and child?" Virgil asked as another man pulled the gun from his belt.

"She is fine for now where she is. I don't want you two getting together and planning some kind of a getaway. Now get out some grub, me and my men are hungry," Ashton told Virgil shaking his gun at him.

Virgil began pulling pans from the wagon and picking up branches for a cook fire. He went about doing what he was told but all the while he was planning something to get out of the mess he was in. All he could think about was the safety of his wife and little Annabel.

Virgil cooked up a slab of side pork and made some biscuits for the outlaws.

"What about the fellow that's keeping watch over my wife? Won't he be hungry too?" Virgil asked trying to figure out just how many of them there were.

"Ain't nobody looking after your wife Hollister, we have her trapped in a cave. There ain't no way she can move that big rock in front of the opening to get out," Billy said feeling proud of his actions.

"She needs some food too Ashton and so does my daughter or have you become so ruthless that you would starve an innocent woman and child?" Virgil said trying to rile Ashton.

"Your wife can feed the baby and she isn't going to starve in one night so shut up and get me some more pork," Billy Ashton snapped.

"Oh but you don't understand, my wife can't feed the baby. She has to use the milk from our goat," Virgil told him.

With that Virgil went to the back of the wagon and produced the goat so Ashton and his men could see the animal.

"Maybe he's telling the truth Billy. I don't mind shooting up a few folks and jumping their claims but I ain't taking no part in killing a little baby," one of the other men with Ashton said.

There were two other men with Billy Ashton and both of them were as filthy and disgusting as Billy himself.

"Shut your mouth Cletus and you keep yours shut, too Jeb," Ashton shouted at his crew.

"Why else would he have a goat in his wagon Billy? I agree with Cletus, I say we let him get that baby some milk and one of us can take it to her. I ain't having no part of a baby starving either Billy," Jeb told him.

"Oh alright, go ahead and fix the youngin' some milk and one of the boys will get it to your wife, but no funny business Hollister or the baby gets nothing. You understanding me boy?" Ashton yelled at Virgil.

Virgil answered, "Yes sir, I understand Mr. Ashton."

He proceeded to get some milk from the goat and poured it into the deer skin that Cassie had made into a feeding bottle for Annabel.

"Think, think," Virgil thought to himself trying to figure out some way of helping his family.

"That'll do Hollister hand it over and quit your stalling," Billy told Virgil.

Virgil handed the bag of milk to Ashton and he gave it to Jeb and said, "You get this to the Hollister woman and then you get right back you hear?"

Jeb nodded his head yes and took the bag and headed off through the trees. That left only two of them watching Virgil and he knew that if he didn't think of something fast his chance to get away would pass.

"I gotta go relieve myself Billy," Cletus said and stood up and walked behind the wagon.

"Where's my pork boy?" Ashton shouted at Virgil.

Virgil picked up the cast iron skillet and walked over to where Billy was sitting on a rock.

"Here you go Mr. Ashton, help yourself," Virgil said.

Just as Billy started to stick his knife in another piece of pork Virgil threw the hot grease from the skillet in his face.

Billy started screaming as the hot grease burned his eyes. When he did Virgil hit him in the head as hard as he could with the flat side of the cast iron skillet.

Cletus jumped from behind the wagon as Virgil grabbed for Billy's gun.

"Come on out here, I got a gun," Virgil yelled.

Cletus walked slowly from behind the wagon with his hands high in the air.

"Don't shoot me mister, I won't try nothing, I swear," the dirty claim jumper begged.

Ashton was still whining in pain from the hot grease and could not see.

"You've blinded me you!" Ashton screamed still trying to wipe the grease from his eyes with his shirt sleeve.

"Serves you right Ashton, serves you right!" Virgil screamed back to him.

"You throw down your gun very slowly and get over here and sit next to Ashton," Virgil instructed Cletus.

Cletus carefully reached for his six shooter but instead of throwing it on the ground he tried to pull it out of the holster and shoot Virgil.

Out of instinct Virgil fired and Cletus fell to the ground dead.

"What happened, Cletus did you get him?" Ashton asked not able to see anything.

"No Billy, he didn't get me, but I got him," Virgil said feeling a little sick. He had never fired a gun at anyone let alone killed a man before.

The sick feeling passed quickly when he thought of his wife and child and he whacked Billy on the back of the neck with the butt of the gun. Billy slumped forward and sprawled out on the ground unconscious. Virgil found some new rope in the wagon and tied Billy's hands and feet so he couldn't get away if he woke up before he returned.

Virgil looked toward the trees and in a low voice said,

"Don't worry Cassie, I'm coming, I'm coming for you honey."

Chapter 9

Virgil raced through the trees but kept as quiet as he could in case the other outlaw was on his way back. Jeb had his own gun and Virgil knew that he would be a better shot. It didn't take long before he heard Jeb tromping through the dry, crunchy leaves and he knew right where he was.

"Hey Jeb," Virgil said trying to sound like Cletus.

"The boss wants you back at the campsite. He's mad as a hornet and says you're taking, too long."

"Oh yeah, well he better watch out cause I'm getting mighty tired of taking orders from him," Jeb said although not loud enough that Ashton would hear him if he could.

"Where are you Cletus? I can't see you for all of this brush and trees," Jeb asked.

"Over here Jeb, I'm over here," Virgil said trying to get Jeb to come to him unknowingly.

Virgil was in a quandary. Did he just shoot an unsuspecting man or capture him and take him back to the authorities? Cassie would never understand killing a man in cold blood no matter what he had done. Virgil waited behind a tree until he saw Jeb pass him and jumped out and stuck the gun barrel in his back.

"Okay friend, you take me to my wife and child or I'll shoot you like I did your buddy," Virgil demanded.

"I heard a gunshot but I thought one of them had shot you," Jeb said trying to sound unconcerned.

"Throw your gun down on the ground nice and slow and don't try any funny business because that's what happened to Cletus," Virgil said.

Jeb pulled his gun from the holster and dropped it on the ground like he was told.

"Okay, start walking," the young Hollister told the claim jumper.

Jeb walked a ways until he came to a large boulder that was up against the opening of a mine.

"She's in there," Jeb told him.

"Grab that tree limb and help me move this rock," Virgil replied.

"Cassie, are you and Anna okay?" he called out to his wife.

"Virgil is that you honey?" Cassie cried out sounding very afraid.

"Yes, you hold on and I'll roll this rock away from the entrance of the mine," he told her.

There was enough space around the boulder to see her and Anna. He could reach in and touch her hand but there was not enough room for her to squeeze her body through.

"Things aren't very stable in here Virg. Rocks from the ceiling keep falling down. Several of them almost hit me and the baby," Cassie called out to him.

About that time a rumbling sound came from the belly of the mine and rocks began falling right inside of the opening. They stopped for just an instant and then all hell broke loose.

The sound of the ceiling caving in and the rocks falling caused a wave of pain through Virgil's heart.

He had forgotten all about Jeb and began yelling his wife's name over and over again.

Finally the sound of the mine collapsing ended and Virgil stood there as white as a ghost staring at Jeb.

"I'm sorry mister, I didn't mean to hurt your wife or baby. I was only doing what Billy told me to," Jeb said.

"Well, Billy Ashton won't be telling you what to do anymore and if you want to spare your soul from the eternal fires of damnation then you will help me dig until I find my wife and baby. So help me God if they are dead I will put a bullet right between your eyes," Virgil said with tears streaming down both cheeks.

Jeb quickly starting pitching rocks away from the mine opening. Virgil knew that if Cassie and the baby were still alive that it wouldn't take long before they would run out of air.

Virgil threw rocks until his hands were a bloody mass. Finally after several hours of steady digging they created a space into the mine so at least Virgil knew that they wouldn't suffocate if they were still alive. Dust came boiling out through the hole they had made and Virgil called her name over and over but there was no reply.

"Have you got a shovel or pick in your wagon Hollister?" Jeb asked.

"Yes I do, I'll go fetch them," Virgil said hurrying back to the campsite.

Jeb thought for a moment about fleeing but decided that after this incident his claim jumping days were over. He hadn't known Billy Ashton for very long and had never been in a lot of trouble. He was just a drifter with no family and no home looking for an easy buck. He had no idea that by hooking up with Billy that he would be putting the life of a young woman and baby in jeopardy.

Jeb running off was the last thing on Virgil's mind. All he wanted was to get to his wife no matter what and Jeb was helping him do that.

When Virgil returned to his campsite he found Billy Ashton moaning in pain and the dead body of Cletus. He rummaged through his wagon until he found his pick and shovel and hurried back to the collapsed cave.

He threw the shovel in Jeb's direction and the two of them began picking and shoveling their way into the mine. The whole time they were working one or the other of them was calling out to Cassie.

"Why are you sticking around to help me?" Virgil finally asked Jeb.

"You know Hollister it is a funny thing. All of a sudden I don't want to be a claim jumper any longer. I'm sorry for your wife and daughter and I feel responsible for their situation and I want to help. I'm not really a bad man. I have never been in real trouble with the law. I got caught up in this when Billy approached me at the saloon in Sacramento and wanted to know if I would like to make some easy money. I should have known that there is no such thing as easy money," Jeb told him.

The two of them were digging as fast as they could when Jeb said, "Listen, do you hear that noise?"

"Yes, it sounds like coughing. It must be Cassie!" Virgil shouted and began picking faster and faster.

"Cassie, Cassie can you hear me?" Virgil cried out into the dark and dusty mine.

Finally they had made an opening large enough for Virgil to climb through and without even thinking of his own safety he was inside the mine.

"I can't see a thing, I need some light," Hollister shouted out to Jeb.

"Will you go fetch me a lantern from the wagon? There is one hanging right inside of the back," Virgil told him.

Jeb took off running through the trees until he reached the wagon. There he saw the body of Cletus and the tied up and badly scalded face of Billy.

"I'll kill you if it's the last thing I do Hollister," Ashton yelled out as he heard Jeb running to the wagon.

"It's not Hollister Billy, its Jeb," his partner replied.

"Did you get Hollister? Did you kill him?" Billy yelled out.

"I'm helping him find his wife and child Billy. They were in the mine when it caved in," Jeb told him.

"Well untie me you idiot and we can still kill him. I want to kill all of them for what they did to me. I can't see anything, he has blinded me!" Ashton cried out.

Jeb reached inside of the wagon and took the lantern.

"Sorry Billy but I'm kind of busy right now," Jeb said as he ran back through the trees.

He could hear Ashton screaming at him as he ran.

"I'll kill you, too you fool. I'll get you all!" Billy hollered.

Jeb couldn't help but smile a little at the thought of a blinded bleeding man threatening his life out in the middle of nowhere.

"I'm back Hollister, here is the lantern," Jeb said holding the lantern inside of the opening.

Virgil struck a match that he had in his pocket and lit the lantern so he could see.

He began making his way through the rocks and the rubble and calling out to his wife. Finally he heard Cassie coughing and gasping for air and he found her clutching to the blanket that held Annabel.

Virgil pulled her closer to the opening and hollered out for help.

"Help me Jeb, I can't carry Cassie while she is holding the baby. I'm afraid she'll drop her," he called out.

Jeb took a few steps into the mine and scooped the baby from Cassie's arms and Virgil picked up his wife and finally they were all safely outside of the cave.

Virgil began wiping the dust and dirt from Cassie's face and begged her to breathe. All at once Virgil realized that the baby was not making any sound. There was no crying coming from the blanket. Cassie coughed a few more times and then finally began breathing normally.

"Where is my baby, where is Anna?" Cassie cried reaching into the air as if Anna was floating before her.

"She is right here honey," Virgil said handing the blanket back to his wife.

Cassie took the bundle and opened the blanket to find Annabel was alive but quiet. She put her up on her shoulder and patted her back rather hard until Anna began to cry.

"Oh thank God," Cassie said as the wailing from the baby was music to her ears.

It was over and Virgil had tears streaming down both cheeks.

Cassie looked up and saw Jeb standing by her husband and yelled, "Look out Virgil!"

"It's okay Cass, he helped me dig you and Anna out of the mine. He helped to save your lives," Virgil said holding a hand out to Jeb.

Jeb shook his hand and looked at Cassie and said,

"I'm sorry ma'am, I'm sorry that I had anything to do with any of this."

"Can you walk Cassie? I think we need to get you and the baby back to the wagon," Virgil said quietly.

"Mr. Hollister, when I went back to get the lantern Ashton was awake and threatening to kill all of us. I thought you might want to know that before you go walking into camp with your wife and daughter," Jeb reported to Virgil.

"Thanks, we'll go back to the edge of the tree line and I'll go in alone to make sure that he is still tied up securely," Virgil said.

"I guess I'll have to take him to the closet town and turn him over to the marshal."

Jeb lowered his head and Cassie looked at him and said,

"If you get on your horse and get away, we might not be able to find you Jeb."

Jeb looked at both of them and said,

"Are you sure? You mean you won't turn me in?"

"Go on and get, I never heard of you. By the way, thanks for helping me," Virgil told him.

Jeb smiled for the first time in many years and tipped his hat and took off for his horse. He was going to turn over a new leaf and find himself a real job and a town to settle down in. Seeing the look of love in Virgil's eyes as he looked at this wife had made a deep impression on Jeb and he wanted to have this feeling himself. He vowed as he rode away that he would never do anything unlawful again. He knew he had received another chance at life and he was not going to waste it.

"I think we have saved three lives here today my dear," Virgil said as he and Cassie watched Jeb ride away.

He pulled his wife and Anna close to him and said,

"I love you Cassie, I love you both so much."

She put her arm around his shoulder and said,

"I wasn't afraid, I knew you would get us out honey."

Chapter 10

Virgil put his hand out to stop Cassie from crossing through the tree line and whispered for her to stay there.

She nodded her head yes and Virgil walked back into the campsite.

Billy Ashton was still tied up but rolling around trying to get his hands loose.

"Who is it?" Billy demanded.

"It's Hollister Mr. Ashton and I'm taking you in," Virgil replied.

"Where's Jeb. I didn't hear any gun shots," Billy said.

Virgil looked at his wife and replied,

"He died in the mine. He went in looking for my wife. She came out but before he could find his way back the mine collapsed so I figure he's dead," Virgil told him.

Cassie nodded her head in approval of the story that her husband told Billy. They both knew that if

Ashton thought Jeb was dead then he would not tell anyone about him or go looking for him if he was ever released from prison.

"It serves the trader right!" Ashton answered.

"You and I are going to find a marshal tomorrow and then you'll get what serves you right Ashton," Virgil told Billy.

"I can't ride anywhere, I can't see," Billy shouted.

"You can ride in the wagon Ashton and I'll have my wife get some grease to put on your eyes. The vision may come back to them after they heal a bit," Virgil told him.

He motioned his wife to come on through the tree line and told her to see if she could find some grease or lard or anything that he could put on Billy's eyes.

Cassie hurried to the wagon and placed Anna in her crib and began looking through their belongings for something to ease Ashton's burning eyes.

"You'd better hope that I don't get my sight back you yellow polecat because if I do I'm going to split you right down the middle like a mule deer," Billy threatened.

"Don't let him bother you Cassie, he's just bluffing. I'm keeping my eye on you Ashton and if you make one uneasy move I'll blow your greedy head off with my shotgun so stop trying to scare my wife," Virgil replied.

"I'm not afraid of him anymore. He is a pathetic worm of a man. Anyone who would put a woman and her baby in a mine shaft is no man at all," Cassie said as she came from around the corner of the wagon.

She handed her husband the jar of axel grease and he walked over to Ashton and wiped it across his burns.

"I'm going to tie this kerchief over your eyes so don't make any sudden moves," Virgil told him.

Billy had tried repeatedly to untie his hands but the rope was too, tight. He knew when he had been licked but in case the opportunity came along he planned to take full advantage of the situation.

Cassie picked up the skillet and put a few strips of salt pork in it and set it over the fire. Virgil pointed at the pan of biscuits he had already made and the two of them had their supper.

"You go ahead and get in the wagon Cass and get some sleep. I'll stand watch over Billy for a few hours and then I'll take my turn in the wagon," Virgil told his wife.

"What about him?" Cassie asked looking at the dead body of Cletus.

"I suppose I'll have to bury him. It seems like I have done a lot of that lately," he said thinking about all of the folks at Heaven's Gate.

"Maybe when we get back to Jackson I'll open up a funeral parlor," Virgil said shaking his head in disgust.

Each of the Hollister's took their turn guarding Ashton through the night and both had taken their turn sleeping for about four hours. The morning sun finally came up over the mountain top and Cassie was preparing some breakfast and making a pot of coffee.

"Wake up Ashton, I'll get you a cup of coffee," Virgil yelled out to his enemy.

He poured some coffee in a tin cup and walked over to where Billy Ashton was laying on the cold hard ground.

"Sit up and I'll take that kerchief off and we'll see if your sight has come back," Virgil told Billy.

Ashton sat upright and Virgil handed the coffee to his tightly tied hands. He removed the scarf from his head and Billy blinked hard a couple of times and said,

"Wipe my eyes, there's grease in them. I don't know if I can see or not."

When Virgil leaned down to wipe his eyes Billy tried to throw the hot coffee up at his face. The scorching hot liquid missed his face as he dodged but hit him in the neck and Virgil let out a yell.

Billy jump up and head butted him and when Virgil fell Billy started kicking him. Even though his feet were tied together he could still kick both boots with tremendous force. Finally a boot made its way to Virgil's head and he lay still.

Cassie grabbed the six shooter from the back of the wagon and without any hesitation fired a shot that went right into Ashton's chest. It was all over as

Ashton rolled his eyes towards Cassie and in his dying breath said,

"Nice yellow dress ma'am."

Cassie ran over to her limp husband and patted his face until he slowly opened his eyes.

"Are you okay Virg?" she asked with a frantic look on her face.

"Yea, I'm okay honey. What happened?" he asked still dazed from the boot that found his head.

"I shot him Virgil. I killed Billy Ashton. He won't be bothering us anymore," she said shaking so hard she dropped the gun.

Virgil looked over and saw the pool of blood running from Ashton's slumped body. He smiled up at her loving face and said, "You did what you had to Cass, nothing wrong with that."

Cassie wrapped her arms around Virgil and began to sob almost uncontrollably.

"I never thought that I could kill anyone Virg, no matter what. I saw you lying there unconscious and all I could think about was not letting him hurt you anymore," Cassie cried.

"You did the right thing honey, its okay there is no need to beat yourself up. Ashton wasn't worried about you or Annabel when he trapped you in that mine. God will not hold this against you Cassie. He knows you are a good woman," Virgil said trying to console her.

"Looks like I have two graves to dig now," Virgil said as he made his way up on his feet.

After the deed of burying the dead was over they loaded up their wagon and headed for Mt. Blackberry. Cassie was holding Anna sitting next to her husband at the front of the wagon like nothing had happened. The only thing that had changed was now they had two more horses tied to the back of the wagon and one of them was the white mare.

"It will be good to have the extra horses Cassie. Now if I need to go for supplies I won't have to take the wagon and I can get there much faster," Virgil stated.

"I will be glad when we finally get our gold and can head home. I don't like this country as much as I thought I did Virgil. I miss my folks and my brothers and sisters," Cassie said as her words tapered off to a quiet sigh.

Virgil looked at her and replied, "Well we have to get enough gold to make the trip home dear. Let's take this one day at a time and we will know the right time to leave. I'm kind of missing my family, too."

He smiled at her and knew that she was still somewhat in shock from all that had happed in the past two days.

It was a warm day and the birds were chirping as they traveled back to Mt. Blackberry and Heaven's Gate.

The wispy clouds in the azure sky created all sorts of objects that would automatically change with the push from a gentle breeze. They would each take a turn pointing out to the other what their minds were conjuring up as they gazed at the ever changing cloud pictures. It made the time pass quickly and kept Cassie from reliving the horrifying events that had occurred the day before. Finally after several hours of traveling through the rocky terrain and steep cliffs they began to recognize their surroundings and knew that they were fast approaching their campsite.

"I think we should arrive at Mt. Blackberry by lunch time. I'm hungry as a bear how about you dear?" Virgil said making small talk.

"I'm hungry too, I'll make us some cornbread and beans for lunch," Cassie said finally feeling better.

She was excited to get back to mining gold and forgetting about Billy Ashton and his attempts of stealing their claim.

The wagon rolled to a stop and they were once again at their campsite. It wasn't long after they had arrived and were busy eating cornbread and beans that a wagon load of people pulled up on their property.

"Howdy do neighbor!" a middle aged gentleman with a pipe protruding from his lips said.

"Howdy!" Virgil answered. "What can I do for you folks?"

"We heard that several families had been headed this way after a long struggle of gold mining. I was told that they were on their way to a settlement about fifty miles from here. We stopped at that settlement but found that they had not arrived. You wouldn't have seen them by any chance?" the stranger asked.

"Do you know any names friend?" Virgil asked hoping that these people were not looking for the folks at Heaven's Gate.

"My daughter Rachel was one of them. Her and her husband left on a wagon train from Missouri over a year ago. There are several families here that are kin folk with those people. We decided to go in search of them and maybe put some roots down in this beautiful country ourselves," a middle aged woman with a pretty smile said.

Cassie's heart sank as she threw a quick glance at Virgil and replied,

"We have met lots of folks out here ma'am. What is your daughter's last name?"

"Bannister is her married name. I know it is a long shot but we have been searching for several weeks now and haven't found hide nor hair of them," the concerned mother told them.

Cassie's eyes immediately went to Annabel and she thought that she could see a resemblance of the woman in the child's face.

"Why don't you folks camp here for the night and get some rest. We have plenty of food and there is a river not far from here," Virgil invited them politely.

Cassie shot him a look that should have punctured his face. Her eyes widened to the size of small saucers and he could see that she was gritting her teeth so hard he was afraid that she would break them all out.

"What do you think mother?" the man driving the wagon asked his wife.

"I'll ask the others, I know I am tired but we will take a vote on it father," the worn out lady answered.

They all agreed to stop for the night and Cassie was so furious at her husband that she threw her plate of beans down on a rock and scooped Anna out of her crib and headed for their wagon.

Virgil followed her and once they were all three inside Cassie began yelling at him in a low voice so the others would not hear her.

"What in the world are you doing Virgil?" Cassie shouted in a whisper.

"They will take Annabel away from us, I couldn't stand that. Don't you love her like your own?" Cassie asked him as she began to weep.

"Of course I do dear, but that lady out there and her husband, they are Annabel's grandparents. They are her rightful kin. Do you think we should lie to them about her? It is going to be hard enough for them to accept that their daughter is dead at least Annabel is a piece of her that they can have to love," Virgil told his crying wife.

"Then we won't tell them about Rachel or the others. They will never know if we keep our mouths shut. They won't get their hearts broken and neither will I," Cassie said as she gulped hard and sniffed away the tears.

"Could you honestly live with yourself Cassie? You could keep that secret from Anna all of her life? What if she found out that she wasn't our child? She would hate us for keeping her away from her rightful family. Cassie I can't do this to them. They have never hurt us they are just looking for their daughter. Think how you would feel if you were those folks," Virgil argued.

Virgil shook his head in despair and jumped out of the back of the wagon to visit with their guests.

Cassie popped her head out before he walked away and said,

"Let me think about this Virgil. Please before you say anything, just let me think about this."

He nodded his head yes and for a moment thought that maybe his wife was right. He loved Anna as if she were his own flesh and blood and how would anyone ever know if they didn't tell. He shook his head again to clear his thoughts and walked over to where the people were climbing from the wagon.

"How did you folks come to this location?" Virgil asked without acting suspicious.

"First let me introduce myself young man. My name is Eldon Gates and this is my lovely wife Prudence. We are from the great state of Missouri. We decided after Rachel had been gone for a year that we would come out and join her and her husband Will. They had sent us a letter about six months ago and told us that they were in the San Francisco area so that is where we went first. Some folks there had met them and the others they were traveling with and said they had all headed in this direction. I hear tell that they may have been on their way to Sacramento but I'm not sure," Mr. Gates told Virgil.

"I see," Virgil said wanting to change the subject.

"Did you bring your whole family Mr. Gates?" Hollister asked.

"Rachel is our only child. Her mother had some difficulties when she was born and the doc back in Missouri said that we probably wouldn't be having anymore. Rachel is our pride and joy and we love her more than anything on God's earth," Eldon Gates told Virgil smiling as if saying his daughter's name made a light shine in his eyes.

Virgil felt a sick feeling in the pit of his stomach. How could he tell these wonderful people that their daughter had been killed by Indians and was buried right across the trec line? How could he tell them that the only part of her left was now a part of his family?

There were a total of eight people with the wagon. Four had been in the back and then the Gates had been riding up front on the buckboard. There were two more, a married couple, that had been walking behind the wagon. They all seemed to be pleasant and well mannered folks.

Cassie finally came out of the wagon but without Anna. She had fed her and had put her down to sleep in her crib.

"Howdy ma'am, didn't you have a baby with you when we drove up?" Mr. Gates asked as he tipped his hat to Cassie.

"Yes, that is Anna, she has a full belly and I put her down for a nap," Cassie replied trying to smile.

"I hope we aren't putting you out dear. If you don't mind my asking why are the three of you out here all by yourselves? Aren't you afraid of Indians or bears?" Mrs. Gates asked Cassie.

All at once the horrifying picture of Rachel laying in her wagon with arrows protruding from her chest entered Cassie's mind.

"Excuse me, I'm not feeling very well. I need to clean up from the mid day meal. I have some beans and cornbread left over, you all are welcome to it if you like," Cassie said not able to look the grandmother in the face.

"Hey, that is right friendly of you. I'll take some of that off of your hands," Eldon replied rubbing his belly.

"Help yourself Mr. Gates," Virgil told him.

"Eldon son, please call me Eldon," Gates said with a grin.

Mr. and Mrs. Gates seemed to take particular interest in Cassie probably because they missed their daughter so much and Cassie was close to her age. It seemed that no matter when she would go in the campsite Prudence Gates was standing right beside her trying to lend a hand or visit.

Annabel started to cry and Cassie hurried to the wagon to hold her. Prudence looked lovingly at the baby and said,

"Oh my dear may I hold her?" I hope one day to be a grandmother myself. She is such a pretty little thing, so delicate and with such big bright eyes."

Cassie handed Annabel over to Mrs. Gates and ran to where Virgil was putting more wood on the fire.

"I can't stand this Virgil, you are right, you always are. We must tell them the truth and let them have Annabel. She belongs to them and she should know the memory of her real mother, it is the right thing to do," Cassie said as she began to weep. She put her hands over her eyes and Virgil enveloped her in his arms.

"Let them have a good night's rest and we will tell them all in the morning. I know it is hard Cass but we will have our own baby one day and you will be glad that you did this," Virgil told her.

"This is the punishment I get for killing that awful Ashton," Cassie sobbed.

"Don't be silly, you are not being punished. Maybe this is God's way of helping Rachel's parents live with the death of their only child," Virgil whispered in her ear.

Cassie looked up at him with tear stained eyes and said,

"Yes Virg, I think you're right. I am feeling better about this now, thank you."

Chapter 11

Everyone sat around the fire that evening and talked and Cassie even managed to conjure up a smile or two. Virgil was so proud of her and he knew that someday soon she would make a wonderful mother. The newcomers all went to bed early and Cassie and Virgil took Anna into their wagon for the last time as a family. They knew that the next morning would be full of grief and tears but they had to do the right thing.

"How are we going to tell them Virgil?" Cassie asked.

"I think I know a way. I will take care of it Cass," Virgil said as he kissed his wife and Anna on the forehead and rolled over to close his eyes for the night.

The Hollister's woke to the sound of bacon frying in a skillet and the smell of biscuits and coffee. Cassie stared at Anna in her wooden crib as if to burn a picture of her on her mind.

"I love you Annabel Hollister, I mean Bannister," Cassie said.

Anna was clapping her tiny hands together and cooing at the sound of Cassie's voice.

"We'd best get up and at'em Cass. We have a lot going on today," her husband told her.

Virgil picked Annabel up and held her close to his chest and said, "You will be someone very special Anna. You have so many that love you so much."

He handed her back to his wife and pulled his trousers on and slipped a clean shirt on over his head.

"I'm going for coffee do you want me to bring you some?'

"No dear, we'll be right out," Cassie said feeling a peace in her heart.

She wrapped the baby in several blankets to keep the chill off of her and stepped out of the wagon and headed for the fire. Their guests were all making a fuss over Annabel and what a beautiful child she was. It was nice to have the company and share a meal with others. They chatted and laughed for over an hour and then Cassie decided that it was time for Virgil to give them all the bad news.

Cassie stood up and with Anna cradled in her arms said,

"My husband has something that he needs to tell you fine people. Please take a seat on a rock or a log and listen to him."

Virgil went over to the wagon and removed the marble plaque that he had made to erect at Heaven's Gate and brought it to the campsite. He had it covered with some bedding so no one would be able to read it until he had finished speaking.

Virgil took a deep breath and then began his speech.

"Dear people, what I am about to tell you is the story of twenty five God fearing, hard working people who decided to make California their home. They were folks from Massachusetts, Missouri and several other states that had a vision of heading west in search of a dream. They had tried their best but in the end realized that their dreams were more about family and faith then that of possessions or gold.

Their fate had been sealed before they ever left their home states but in the year and a half that they spent in California they had a unique adventure and became a loving and happy community. These folks were on their way to founding a new town that they could call their own when they had to stop because a new life could not wait to join them. During this time God took them all at the hands of some renegade Indians. He took all but one," Virgil said as he held his hands out to Cassie for the baby.

"This beautiful child is the sole survivor of that Indian raid and her name is Annabel Bannister. She is the daughter of Will and Rachel Bannister."

Virgil pulled the cover from the plaque and let the families read what had been forever etched into the marble.

"I buried every one of those people myself and my wife Cassie and I prayed for all of them. I had this monument made in Sacramento to place at the site where these people were laid to rest. We decided to call it Heaven's Gate and that is why that name appears on the plaque," Virgil told them.

Prudence Gates sat there quiet as did all of the others. These people were their children and family members he was telling them about. Virgil walked over to Mrs. Gates and handed Annabel to her and said,

"Mrs. Gates this is your granddaughter, her name is Annabel. That is the name Rachel had given her."

"That is my middle name," the shocked woman replied.

She took the baby in her arms and rocked her back and forth until the tears finally came. She did not wail or cry out loud there were only quiet tears, some of joy for this child she held and some in grief for her lost daughter.

"Would some of you men help me carry this plaque over to the resting place of your loved ones?" Virgil asked.

All of the men walked over to help Virgil carry the heavy monument through the tree line where their kin had been buried.

"Would one of you be so kind as to bring a shovel?" Virgil asked.

The women stayed sitting around the fire and the men went to erect the monument that Virgil had so unselfishly purchased in Sacramento.

Finally Cassie saw her husband standing in the tree line and without a word spoken all of the women walked to where they had erected the plaque.

The mounds of dirt were everywhere they looked and there was no way that any of them knew where their loved one had been placed. One by one each of the ladies rubbed their hand across the cool and white marble plaque. Finally Prudence Gates said,

"God bless you young man for all that you have done. Then she turned and looked at Cassie and said,

"God bless you also for taking such good care of my granddaughter. I have only one question about all of this. Where were you when the Indians killed the others?"

Cassie walked up to Mrs. Gates and with all of them standing close she and Virgil told the story of Mt. Blackberry and why they had been up on the mountain when the attack came.

"I understand, thank you," Mrs. Gates said still seeming to be in a state of shock.

They all walked very quietly back across the tree line and to the Hollister's campsite. Prudence sat down by Cassie and asked specific questions about the Indian raid and without being graphic Cassie told her the entire story of how she found Annabel wiggling under the blanket.

"You saved my grandchild Mrs. Hollister, how can I ever repay you?" Mrs. Gates asked.

"I fell in love with her ma'am. It was no trouble at all. Virgil and I had planned to raise her as our own. I must admit that I will miss her very much but I know that she belongs with her kin and that she is not mine to raise," Cassie told her.

The whole time Cassie and Mrs. Gates were talking Virgil and Eldon Gates were having their own conversation.

"Do you plan on going back east now that you have found your granddaughter Eldon?" Virgil asked him.

Mr. Gates thought a moment and then stood up and said so all could hear,

"Friends, we have found out some astonishing news today and the time has come for us decide whether we are going back east or staying on in California. The death of our loved ones has changed our plans. Who wants to stay and who thinks we should go back? I think that we should take a vote and the majority should rule. What say ye?" Mr. Gates asked.

"Let us talk it over Eldon," one of the family members said.

The six other people began discussing the matter and then Virgil stood up and said,

"Why don't you stay with us? You can start a settlement right here and help us mine our gold. We will share the profits with you and you will be close to your loved ones.

I have a deed to this land. I filed a claim in Sacramento several weeks ago. I own this mountain and Heaven's Gate. There is plenty of timber to build homes and the river is here. We could start our own community and the profits from the gold would pay for everything. What do you think Cass?" Virgil asked excited about his idea.

Cassie thought about her family in Jackson and then she looked at Annabel. She was torn between going home and staying with the child she had grown to love so much.

The eight guests began buzzing amongst themselves and in only a few moments agreed that they would be willing to put down roots in Heaven's Gate.

"We have given up our homes and have come out west to start a new life. We have nothing to go back to so if you want us to stay we will," Eldon Gates told the Hollister's.

"What do you say Cass? You told me you thought this country was beautiful. I would have help mining the gold and you can help raise Anna. It is a perfect solution for everyone. With these men here there is no telling how much gold we can dig from the mountain and we would be better prepared if the Indians came back," Virgil stated.

Cassie kept looking at Annabel and then said,

"Could we go back someday if I wanted to? After we mined enough gold to live on could we go home?"

"Whatever you want dear," Virgil said hoping she would approve of the idea.

"All right then, let's do it Virgil," she said with a smile.

They all began to cheer and what had started out as the worse day of their lives became the start of a new beginning for them all.

Virgil began telling the men about the mine and how to get to it and the women all started sharing their dreams of a church and a school house. It wasn't long before the men had the mining business running like a well oiled clock. They had devised a plan of digging deep into the mountain and placing timbers as they went to hold up the walls to prevent them from collapsing.

Weeks turned into months and Cassie and Prudence had become as close as mother and daughter. The men would take turns riding by two's to the nearest town and turning their gold nuggets and dust into cash. Once every three months Virgil and Eldon would hitch up the wagon and would go to Sacramento and buy flour, sugar, nails, building supplies and whatever they needed to live.

They made friends with the suppliers and more people came to Heaven's Gate to start their families and the town began to flourish. In only a short time the town's population had grown to almost fifty people of all ages. Their dream was becoming a reality and Cassie and Virgil were as happy as they had ever been.

They had been saving their money in a bank in Sacramento and although they were sharing the profits from the mine with four other couples they were finally getting ahead.

Annabel was growing like a weed and Prudence and Cassie took turns playing with her and caring for her. Annabel thought of Prudence as her mama and Cassie as her big sister. One of the women from Boston had been a school teacher and the ladies all decided it was time to start some formal schooling at Heaven's Gate. There were several families who had children and they needed to learn to read and write.

They started the school in the teacher's home but soon they had convinced their husbands to build a schoolhouse. They had no need for a sheriff or any city officials when they had started the town but soon it became apparent that there had to be some sort of law and order overseeing Heaven's Gate.

A stage stop had been built about ten miles from the town and coaches began dropping off mail and people were getting news from their families. It wasn't long before more businesses were raised and more homes were built. The people seemed to be coming in droves to live in Heaven's Gate.

One day while sweeping the floor of their three room log home Virgil looked at Cassie and said,

"Did you ever think we would end up like this dear? Starting our own town and having such a fine home?" he asked.

Cassie smiled at him and said,

"I'm glad that I listened to you Virgil. You are right, you are always right and I am blessed to have such a smart man."

He went to her and started to kiss her forehead when they heard someone screaming at the top of their lungs,

"Indians, run for your lives Indians are coming!"

A look of terror streaked across Virgil's face and he told Cassie to stay inside and lock the door. He took the rifle from its perch over the stone fireplace and ran out into the yard.

Men with guns were running in all directions but did not seem to have a plan of where they were going.

"Virgil, what shall we do?" cried Eldon Gates who lived next door to the Hollister's.

"I think we should send the women and children to the schoolhouse or the church and have them lock themselves in for safe keeping," Eldon shouted to his neighbor.

"No, they could set fire to the building and kill them all at one time if we did that. Keep your families in their own homes for now. Follow me Eldon!" Virgil yelled at his neighbor.

Most of the people that were born in the area at least knew a little about fighting Indians but the folks from the east had no idea of what to do and were panic stricken.

Eldon did as he was told and as he ran behind Virgil he cried to the other men to follow as well and they all did. Virgil stopped at the tree line where he could see the Indians riding their painted ponies into town yelping and screaming then the arrows began to fly. Virgil instructed the townsmen to start shooting and draw their attackers away from their homes and town. When the bullets began to fire the Indians raced towards the sound and the men hid behind the trees.

"Okay men, it is time to get your revenge for what started this town in the first place. It is time to show these Indians that we are not a group of helpless farmers from the east but frontiersmen who can fight and take care of what is rightfully ours," Virgil stated as he began firing his rifle.

The sound of Vigil's voice and the words that he spoke sent a sense of pride running through the veins of all of the men and they began shooting and protecting what they had built.

There were more Indians than there were townsmen but it was easier to hit your target with a rifle and then duck behind a tree than racing towards your enemy on horseback out in the open with only bows and arrows.

The Indians began to fall quickly and as the arrows ripped through the air only a few men were hit and none of them fatally. Finally, after losing over half of their war party, the Indians retreated and left their dead scattered along the tree line.

The men of Heaven's Gate had won and they were thankful that none of their own had been killed.

"I don't think they will be coming back men. We have proven to them and to ourselves that we are brave and can take care of our families and our town. I am proud of all of you," Virgil said as they all came out from behind the trees.

"Who is going to bury all of these Indians?" asked Eldon.

Virgil shook his head and said,

"I don't know Eldon but it is not going to be me. I have buried enough people to last me a lifetime."

Chapter 12

The women and children met their husbands and fathers in the street as they came back from the battle to assess their injuries. They were elated to find that not one of their men had been fatally wounded.

Cassie and Prudence doctored the few that had been struck by the flying arrows and the rest of the men loaded the bodies of the fallen Indian braves in a wagon and took them several miles from their town. They may have not have been white men but they were still men and they deserved to be buried the same as any other man who lost his life in battle.

When the last grave was covered Eldon Gates said a few words as the others bowed their heads.

"Dear Father, we ask that these men find peace and their way to You in heaven. Amen."

The townsmen had no way of knowing but behind a hill hid two young Indian boys witnessing the entire burial and prayer. They returned to the Indian village and told their elders of what they had seen and the leader of the tribe, Flying Hawk, felt compassion for the people of Heaven's Gate.

He held a tribal council and told of the kind deed that the white people had done for his warriors and said,

"We will no longer inflict battle on these white settlers. They have shown that they have good hearts by seeking peace with The Great Spirit for our dead in the afterlife. We shall learn to live as one with them. We shall trade and smoke the pipe with their leader and help each other through times of trouble."

Several weeks had passed when Virgil was riding the white mare, Spirit, through the cemetery in Heaven's Gate. His mind was recalling all that he and Cassie had gone through to get where they were now. Virgil heard the sound of a horse walking slowly behind him and when he turned to see who it was he was startled to see a strong and regal looking Indian sitting on a spotted pony behind him His head was covered in long and multicolored feathers. He had on his chest an armor of red, yellow and green beads. His feet were in beaded moccasins and he carried no weapons.

Virgil's first reaction was to pull his gun and fire but as he looked closely at the majestic face of the proud man on horseback his fear left him. There was a peaceful look about the Indian and Virgil held his hand out to him.

The magnificent Indian did the same and they shook hands as if to say hello to one another as equal men. The Indian slid from his pony's back and Virgil dismounted as well.

They couldn't speak the other ones language but in this moment it didn't seem necessary. The Indian floated his hand through the air as if to acknowledge all of the people that were buried around them. Virgil nodded his head yes and Flying Hawk pounded his fist to his chest and dropped his head as if to say that from his heart he was truly sorry for what had happened here. Virgil and Flying Hawk took each other's forearm and that was their sign of friendship and forgiveness. Virgil looked hard into the eyes of the Indian and said,

" Hollister," as he placed his hand on his own chest.

Then Virgil placed his hand on the Indian's chest and about that time the sound of a hawk calling out as he flew overhead was heard by both men. The Indian pointed to the bird in flight and Virgil nodded yes as if he knew that his name was Flying Hawk.

The Indian said,

"Hollister," and Virgil shook his head yes and then replied,

"Flying Hawk."

It was as if some greater power had been there to interpret for each of them. It was a wonderful feeling for both of them to know that there would no longer be any confrontation between their two people. They smiled, nodded their heads and then mounted their horses and went in separate directions. Virgil could hardly wait to get back to town and tell everyone what he had just encountered. The sun seemed to be shining brighter and the air smelled cleaner and fresher. He felt safe but most of all he finally felt like he was home.

Virgil rode back through the tree line, down the main road of town and to the hitching post that stood in front of his house. The logs that made up his house seemed to be straighter and more uniform in their placement. He looked around and the colors of every flower were more vivid and he felt a peacefulness that he had ever felt before. A smile came across his lips and he knew that something wonderful had just happened and he couldn't wait to tell his wife.

Cassie saw him in the yard stroking Spirit and she could tell that he had experienced some sort of an epiphany. She opened the door and walked to his side and said,

"What is it Virgil? Something has happened to you, I can see it in your face."

"Yes Cass, I just had the most incredible experience with Flying Hawk. He is the leader of the Indians that attacked us several weeks ago," he answered.

"Oh my stars, are you all right? Did he hurt you Virgil?" she asked with a concerned voice.

"No, nothing like that Cassie. I was sitting on Spirit at the cemetery and I heard someone coming up behind me. It was this beautiful and powerful looking red man. We reached our hands out to each other and he apologized to me for the attack on all of the folks that were buried there. He didn't say any words but I knew what he was telling me. I told him my name and he told me his. It was as if God and nature was our translator. It was wonderful Cassie. We will never have to worry about them again. I think we are their friends now. I don't know why or how it happened but I think we have made friends with the Indians," Virgil told her looking like he was in a trance.

Tears welled up in Cassie's eyes and she put her arms around the man she had loved all of her life.

"I guess we shouldn't question any of this we should just relish in the mere wonder of it Virg," she said softly in his ear.

Virgil only nodded his head yes and then said,

"We must tell the others. I don't want anyone to take a shot at one of them in case they come back. It was like we made a peace treaty between our people and their people without a spoken word."

Cassie smiled and the two of them walked into the main part of town. There had been a bell erected next to the schoolhouse and Virgil began pulling on the rope and the chiming of the bell rang out so everyone could hear. The town folk came quickly to see what the emergency was.

When everyone was in the street Virgil began telling of his encounter with Flying Hawk. The sound of his voice was the only noise that could be heard. When Virgil had finished Eldon began to clap his hands and soon everyone was applauding. They could tell from the look on Virgil Hollister's face that he had spiritually changed.

The buzzing began among the residents of Heaven's Gate and Cassie said,

"This must surely be the gateway to heaven Virgil. I am content to live here with you now for as long as you want. We never have to go back to Mississippi again."

"We never have to go back?" Virgil asked excited.

"I have been writing to my parents Virgil. I have told them what a wonderful place this was and about all of the fine folks that live here as well. They are tired of their hard lives in the south and they sent word that they are coming here next summer to live. I hope to have a surprise for them shortly after they arrive," Cassie told him.

"What kind of a surprise Cass?" Virgil asked her confused.

"I would like to have my mother here when Virginia Ann comes into this world or Virgil Andrew, whichever it may be," Cassie said grinning.

All at once it hit him what Cassie was talking about and he picked her up and began to swing her around.

"Oh, I'm sorry, did I hurt you honey?" Virgil said as he carefully landed her feet back on the ground. He hugged her tight and then started jumping around like a jack rabbit.

"I'm going to be a father!" he shouted so everyone could hear. The men began to congratulate him and the women started to make a fuss over Cassie.

"This has been the best day of my life," Virgil shouted as the men patted him on the back.

He stopped in his tracks and looked at his loving wife and said,

"What shall we do if the mine runs out of gold Cassie? That is the only living I have here. We are not rich and I don't have enough saved to give you all of the things that you have always dreamed about."

Cassie smiled at him and said,

"Virgil, look around you. You are richer than anyone else I know. You have neighbors that would fight for you. You have friends that love and trust you like you were family."

She took his hand and placed it on her slightly swollen tummy and said,

"I have all the gold I will ever need right here Virgil Hollister."

THE END

Sunflower
Prairie
Publications

Please visit Barbara Sue at her website:

barbarasuesweetwood.weebly.com

She loves to hear from her readers.

All of her books are available at:

Amazon.com or Createspace E-Store

and can be purchased through her website

in paperback or Kindle.

Thank You!

37384272R00096

Made in the USA
Charleston, SC
08 January 2015